OHANA SUNRISE

MAUI ISLAND SERIES BOOK 5

KELLIE COATES GILBERT

Copyright © 2022 by Kellie Coates Gilbert

All rights reserved.

No part of this book may be reproduced in any form or by any electronic or mechanical means, including information storage and retrieval systems, without written permission from the author, except for the use of brief quotations in a book review.

Ohana Sunrise is a work of fiction. Names, characters, places, and incidents are either the product of the author's imagination or are used fictitiously, and any resemblance to actual persons, living or dead, is coincidental.

Cover design: Elizabeth Mackay

For my Gilbert Girls team.
You gals bless me with your early read-throughs, your eagle eyes that identify missed errors, your thoughtful input on storylines and all the reviews you post on social media and on the retailers. Thank you from the bottom of my heart!

PRAISE FOR KELLIE'S BOOKS

"If you're looking for a new author to read, you can't go wrong with Kellie Coates Gilbert."
~**Lisa Wingate**, NY Times bestselling author of *Before We Were Yours*

"Well-drawn, sympathetic characters and graceful language"
~**Library Journal**

"Deft, crisp storytelling"
~**RT Book Reviews**

"I devoured the book in one sitting."
~**Chick Lit Central**

"Gilbert's heartfelt fiction is always a pleasure to read."
~**Buzzing About Books**

"Kellie Coates Gilbert delivers emotionally gripping plots and authentic characters."

~**Life Is Story**

"I laughed, I cried, I wanted to throw my book against the wall, but I couldn't quit reading."
~**Amazon reader**

"I have read other books I had a hard time putting down, but this story totally captivated me."
~**Goodreads reader**

"I became somewhat depressed when the story actually ended. I wanted more."
~**Barnes and Noble reader**

ALSO BY KELLIE COATES GILBERT

THE MAUI ISLAND SERIES
Under The Maui Sky

Silver Island Moon

Tides of Paradise

The Last Aloha

Ohana Sunrise

THE PACIFIC BAY SERIES
Chances Are

Remember Us

Chasing Wind

Between Rains

THE SUN VALLEY SERIES
Sisters

Heartbeats

Changes

Promises

LOVE ON VACATION SERIES
Otherwise Engaged

All Fore Love

TEXAS GOLD SERIES

A Woman of Fortune

Where Rivers Part

A Reason to Stay

What Matters Most

-

STAND ALONE NOVELS

Mother of Pearl

* * *

Available at all retailers

www.kelliecoatesgilbert.com

OHANA SUNRISE
MAUI ISLAND SERIES, BOOK 5

Kellie Coates Gilbert

1

In the mornings, after straightening her bed and taking a quick shower, Ava Briscoe liked to take her cup of hot coffee out onto the lanai, where she'd sit and watch the sunrise. In those quiet early morning hours, she loved to watch the horizon turn lavender, then pink, and finally drift into a light apricot color.

Few things offered more immense pleasure than the faint smell of plumeria, pineapple, eucalyptus, the cheerful chorus of Apapane and I'iwi birds, and the softness of morning before the day began with all of its demands.

Lately, her morning interludes had been abruptly cut short by the arrival of slow-moving machinery and the loud grinding of diesel motors, followed by booming shouts of workers yelling instructions over the noisy grating gears of equipment chugging across the grounds of Pali Maui, her beloved pineapple plantation.

Not that she was complaining. She was more than thankful for the activity. But she now had to get up much earlier if she wanted to enjoy her peaceful time in the morning.

It had been a little over two months since the big storm had blown across Maui, creating chaos and damage across the island. Pali Maui had taken a severe hit with downed trees and flooding. Landscaping had to be replaced. Jon's restaurant roof had to be replaced and interior damage restored. Likewise, the offices and the gift shop needed restoration. The golf course renovation had been markedly hindered. Tom Strobe and his crew's progress had been essentially obliterated by flooding water. The entire design process had to be started over, considering the altered terrain. It would now be months before the project turned any profit.

Worse, a power outage had allowed feral pigs to breach their electric fencing. In hours, the native boars had consumed a vast portion of the pineapple fields, obliterating their harvest.

All this had placed Pali Maui under severe financial stress.

Ava stopped to admire her newly replaced hibiscus bush before making her way to a lounge chair by the pool. She sat and gazed out over the landscape, still muted with a bit of darkness.

Like every morning, she immediately contemplated ways to tighten their monetary belts until cash flow could be restored to a healthy level. It had taken some financial gymnastics to keep Pali Maui afloat. For now, they had the resources to move forward, thanks to each one of them liquidating assets and bolstering their balance sheet, including her brother, Jack.

Currently, they were on a narrow footbridge. Any misstep could send the entire operation plummeting into the chasm of liquidation in order to meet their obligations, essentially closing down Pali Maui.

Attorneys and financial advisors, including her daughter, Christel, advised that chapter eleven bankruptcy, where the court forced debtors to discount what was owed to help restructure liabilities, might be an option. The truth was, Ava, didn't want to go there. Not if she didn't have to. She always paid her bills in full and on time. That was not going to change as long as she had any say in the matter.

Tom Strobe had graciously offered to discount his contract fee. She'd firmly resisted and declined the proposal. For many reasons...the least of which was her firm belief that a good business owner did not mix business with personal friendships. Doing so only invited issues.

Tom argued when she had explained her position. Even so, she stuck to her guns. Just because she'd run into some cash flow issues did not negate the wisdom of maintaining solid boundaries. Besides, the forced delays had already impacted Tom and his business, causing the need to reassess his schedule. She overheard him on a call the other day explaining to a potential client that he could not accept new commitments right now. When he hung up, she urged him to terminate his obligations to her. He wouldn't hear of it. "I'm here and will see this through, Ava. It's important to me."

She and Tom had easily formed a friendship, one she greatly appreciated. Few men were so easy to be around, so gracious and interesting.

The truth was, she saw something in his eyes that suggested he might want more than mere friendship.

The idea that he was attracted to her was unsettling, yet flattering.

Tom Strobe was definitely appealing. Despite his strong profile with a solid square face, straight nose, and chiseled features, there was a warmth to his face. His blue eyes seemed to see things others missed. He was kind, thoughtful, and generous. They shared deep discussions about literature, music, and art, World War II trivia, American history, and the future of politics and its effect on the commodities market...and of course, they both loved to discuss golf.

Amend that to mean they *argued* about golf. Tom was adamant that Tiger Woods would make another comeback and top the leader boards again. She'd laughed at the idea. "Nah, he's over. Not only is Tiger physically challenged by compounded injuries, but his bad choices and actions have robbed him of public favor. His mental game is in the sandpit."

Tom reacted with a fist pound to the table. "You're wrong, Ava. You wait and see."

Remembering all that made her smile, even now.

Ava had been single a little over a year, and the status was not of her choosing. She'd been married for many years before losing her husband to an accident, only to learn in the aftermath that she'd lost him to another woman much earlier.

Her tendency would be to put up walls and never trust another man...or trust herself to choose another man. What did it say about her that she'd never even seen a sign of Lincoln's infidelity prior to the accident?

Then she met Tom and her conviction to remain clear of romantic attachments grew wobbly.

Yes, Tom would be tempting if she weren't still feeling vacant inside. She should be thrilled that a man like Tom was interested in her...because, clearly, he was. Instead, she was sad.

She would never admit this to anyone, but in the deepest part of her, she carried a secret. The truth was, Ava knew she was empty and had nothing to give. Lincoln's death and infidelity, Alana's illness, and the losses at Pali Maui...well, it was too much.

While not a breakdown in the clinical sense, that day on the beach had scared her. She'd felt a darkness that was foreign and alarming. She'd slipped into someone she didn't even recognize. No longer was she the woman in control, the woman who had it all together and was there for everyone. Suddenly, she felt like a wounded puppy and cowered at the notion of experiencing any more hurt.

Relationships could be sticky...even risky. What if things

didn't work out with Tom as hoped? Opening up to another gut punch might take her under. She might not survive another hit.

Tom deserved more than a romantically hollow woman.

Ava lifted her chin and stood, gathering her coffee mug. She turned for the house, knowing that while she appreciated Tom's intentions, it was best just not to go there.

CHRISTEL STEPPED from the shower and reached for the towel. Standing at the mirror shaving, Evan dropped his razor, plucked the thick bath sheet from the rack, and wrapped it around her torso.

"If I didn't have surgery in an hour, I'd scoop up my wife and return to bed," he taunted.

She grinned back at him. "I wonder if Mrs. Peabody knows she's messing with our sex life?" she quickly said in retort. "But far be it from me to keep my former school teacher in pain."

It was a little joke between them that Mrs. Peabody's ailments paid for his entire malpractice bill. She had a hip replacement, a knee replacement, and now, she complained that her ankle was going out. After delivering dozens of steroid shots to alleviate the pain and swelling, Evan had finally determined that an ankle fusion was in order. He would use screws and plates this morning to fixate her bones internally. Christel had not learned this confidential patient information from her husband...but directly from Mrs. Peabody, who kept her hostage in the grocery line last week recounting every ailment she'd suffered in the past two years.

Evan laughed and leaned in and nuzzled her neck. "Raincheck?" he offered.

Christel let herself smile. "It's a date."

She got dressed while he finished shaving. When he gave

her another kiss and bid her goodbye, she pasted a smile and told him she'd see him that evening.

As soon as she knew he was gone, she opened her bathroom drawer and withdrew the box, one of three remaining. Using her fingernail, she carefully lifted the glued flap on the end of the long thin box and slid the test stick from its cellophane packaging.

Christel grinned. She didn't need to read the instructions. This wasn't the first test. It was her third. She only hoped this would not be her third disappointment.

Buoyed with optimism, Christel followed the directions, already anticipating exactly how she might break the good news to Evan. Months back, when he'd first disclosed that he wanted to start a family, she'd initially been reluctant...and more than a little surprised. She shouldn't have been shocked, she supposed. Evan lost his fiancé in a military helicopter accident in Marseilles. Beyond mourning the loss of Tess, he had to let go of plans for a family.

She, too, had been forced to push pause on the idea of children. Jay's addiction had put everything on hold. There was no way she could take on caring for babies while managing her former husband's behavior. It'd taken a lot of counseling and personal reflection to realize she had to release her efforts and let Jay go. Her sanity required such a painful decision.

Her marriage to Evan had provided a fresh start...and new hope on many fronts. After so much heartache and disappointment, she'd finally agreed it was time to start the family they both wanted. They had earned some good news.

She pulled the tiny white plastic wand up where she had a clear view of the small result window and held her breath while searching for the tell-tale pink line.

Her heart sunk when she found none.

Perhaps she'd done the test wrong, she told herself. She grabbed the handle, opened the bathroom drawer, and pulled another test out. Over the course of the following minutes, she repeated the process.

While she waited the requisite time, her mind rehearsed all she'd been through over the past weeks. The storm and its impact on Pali Maui had buried her under a burden that only she truly understood. She was the chief financial officer. Her family depended on her legal and accounting knowledge to maneuver them through this mess. But what was she to do? Could she make it rain money?

Christel took a deep breath and drew the wand up. She opened her eyes.

Again...nothing.

Unbid tears formed. Her heart sunk. Immediately, she felt that horrible wave of letdown.

Worse, she'd have to let Evan down.

Again.

2

Ava refreshed her mug with some hot coffee before heading out for the family meeting she'd called. Since the storm, they'd been meeting weekly to go over progress with the rebuild and issues that seemed to come up unexpectedly. Running Pali Maui had always required commitment and time. Now, it took an all-hands-on-deck approach and countless hours. None of them was excused from providing feedback and helping to develop a strategy for moving forward.

Katie greeted as Ava entered the small conference room. "Morning, Mom." A glance around the room told her everyone was there but one.

"Where's Christel?" she asked, moving to take her seat at the table.

Aiden straightened the stack of papers in front of him. "She must be running late." He glanced at his watch. "And, I don't want to be. Can we get started? I need to get to the station." Aiden was a staunch believer in setting the example as captain. His team at Maui Emergency Services could count on him to 'walk the talk,' as he liked to call it.

Ava nodded. "Yes, let's get started. I'm sure Christel will be here soon."

Over the following minutes, they discussed the grand re-open of No Ka 'Oi. Ava's son-in-law, Jon, was known for marrying the resources of the land and sea into his culinary craft. Both tourists and natives anxiously awaited an opportunity to dine on his cuisine again.

"We're all set for Saturday," Jon reported. "Staffing is still a bit short. We lost a couple of waiters when forced to do a temporary lay-off. Even so, I think we'll be fine."

"It'll be great to get some income on the books," Ava told them. "We're looking to at least nine more months before another pineapple harvest. Until then, we'll be solely dependent on our cash assets."

Aiden frowned. "Any word on insurance?"

Ava ran her finger around the rim of her coffee mug. "As you know, the insurance company has declined coverage. They are taking the position that the storm damage prompted an 'act of God' exclusion."

"Can't we fight them on that?" Shane demanded. "I mean, what about our business interruption addendum?"

When Aiden cocked his head and gave him a look, Shane quickly added, "What? Christel said we had that."

Ava couldn't help but smile. "I think you mean our crop insurance addendum. Yes, that will be paid, but the limits are low. Of course, it will help, but that alone won't solve our problem."

"The real difficulty is their assertion of contributory negligence. They claim our fencing system was faulty, and that was the real reason for the loss," Christel explained as she entered the room and took her place at the table. "We've enlisted a law firm to help us with that." She lifted an orange from the fruit bowl and started peeling. "Sorry I'm late."

It had been everything they could do to keep meeting

payroll so that the entire acreage destroyed by the feral pigs could be replanted. Because growing pineapples was so dependent on replanting the crowns, they had to pay an exorbitant amount to ship starts in from Costa Rica. The outlay had nearly zeroed out their cash on hand.

Because of that, each of them had made significant sacrifices. To raise much-needed capital, Christel mortgaged her beachfront home in Pa'ia. Katie and Jon liquidated their retirement accounts, despite huge penalties. Aiden and Shane both had their houses up for sale. Ava had emptied all her personal accounts, certificates of deposit, and stocks...then

liquidated all assets of any value, including her jewelry collection.

She chastised herself for throwing Lincoln's ring overboard and into the sea after discovering his infidelity. The piece was worth many tens of thousands. She could use that money now.

Unknown to almost everyone on the island, her brother, Jack, was quite wealthy. His tourist business had flourished over the years, and he spent little, except for his bar bill down at The Dirty Monkey. He would have helped more and come to her rescue, but the storm had severely damaged his fleet of boats. He, too, had to rebuild.

Of no surprise, her sister was the opposite. When Ava told Vanessa she would have to pay rent for the shanty she lived in and cover the utilities, her sister had thrown a fit. "I can't possibly pay for all that. My job at the campaign headquarters requires me to maintain a certain image. Much of what I earn goes to my clothing and makeup budget. Do you know what just one Tory Burch bag costs?"

Ava closed the lid of her laptop and stood. She moved for the Keurig machine, where she positioned her mug on the base, then popped a K-cup pod in and pressed the button. "Look, kids...I want you to know how I appreciate everyone's willingness to get us through this financial spot. We Briscoes are a strong bunch, and you've just proved that to be true."

Ava fought the urge to tear up. She swallowed back the emotion, determined to keep this meeting on a professional level.

"I assure you. We will recover from this setback. Christel and I are identifying and instituting measures to protect us from future business upheaval. We'll come out of this even stronger, more adept. I promise."

"Mom, I guess this might be a great time to disclose what I have in the works." Katie's face grew bright with anticipation. She opened her briefcase, pulled a file folder out, and opened it. "In addition to our daily tours, Pali Maui will offer weekly outdoor concerts. The gift shop will sell tickets, including admission, a red checked blanket, and a picnic basket filled with items made in Jon's kitchen. The landscaping renovation will be complete by next week, and we'll hold the concerts in the area below the restaurant. Local musicians will offer their services for free, and Aunt Vanessa helped me secure a PR company that was also willing to discount their marketing fees. She finagled a great deal for us."

Katie looked up expectedly. "Well? What do you think?"

"Depends on the numbers."

They all turned to Christel who reached for the documents on the table and studied them for several seconds. "These proformas look good." Finally, she looked up and smiled over at her sister. "I mean it. Ticket sales will bring in weekly cash with very little outlay or expense. We can limit marketing to social media, which can be very effective and cost very little." She nodded. "I like it."

Katie beamed. "I hoped you would."

It warmed Ava's heart to see her children working together to get Pali Mali on stable financial ground again. They'd all rallied as a family creating a formidable team. The terrible storm damage had opened opportunities for her kids to reach for their individual talents. They were no longer the young adults who too often squabbled and argued. They had to grow up—fast. Christel, Aiden, Katie, and Shane all had to join forces and collaborate.

This effort would prepare them to take over Pali Maui someday, when she could no longer be at the helm.

Her lips lifted in a slight smile.

Her Pali Maui would be in good hands.

3

When the meeting was over, Ava headed to Mig's house to drop off some bills of lading for incoming shipments of pineapple crowns they expected to arrive later in the week. Usually, Mig would be out in the fields at this time of the day. All of their routines had been interrupted in the aftermath of the storm.

She had to knock twice before he answered.

"Hey, Ava...come on in." He waved her inside.

Wimberly Ann was sitting on the sofa. She stood. "Ava! You're just in time. Mig and I were sitting down to today's episode of *The Young and the Restless*. Jack Abbott is about to decipher a cryptic message from Victor Newman, a message which will change Nikki's life forever." She looked to Mig. "Isn't that right, honey peaches?"

Mig shifted on his feet, looking a bit embarrassed.

Wimberly Ann waved them both over to the couch. "Hurry, you don't want to miss the big moment." She pointed the remote at the television screen across the room and turned the sound back on.

"I didn't mean to interrupt," Ava said, trying to hide her smile.

Mig reached for the documents. "No, no, you didn't. Interrupt, I mean."

"Are you sure? Because..." She noticed a slight smudge of pink on his collar. "I can come back later."

Mig ran his other calloused hand through the top of his black hair. "No, you're good."

Ava couldn't help it. The corners of her lips lifted into a tiny grin. "I should be going." She nodded toward the papers in Mig's hand. "Just look those over and alert me if you see any issues with the timing of the deliveries."

He assured her that he would.

Ava turned to go.

"You're not staying?" Wimberly Ann asked from her position on the couch. Her voice was filled with disappointment. "We could fix some popcorn. This soap is really getting good."

"Thanks, but I am on my way to see Alani," Ava explained. "Maybe another time."

"Okay," Wimberly Ann said, barely pulling her eyes from the television. "Tootles."

Minutes later, Ava was in her car and making the half-hour drive to Wailea.

Elta Kané was pastor of Wailea Chapel, a community of faithful congregants who met in a quaint and picturesque white church with a steeple and bell and colorful stained-glass windows. Plush tropical foliage with sweet-smelling plumeria, hibiscus, and Curcuma lined the walkway.

The seaside chapel stood on a bluff overlooking the meticulously kept grounds of Grand Wailea Resort and was a sought-after wedding venue because of the awe-inspiring and romantic setting.

Elta's wife, Alani, was Ava's closest friend. They'd been through a lot together, both happy and sad. Most recently, their friendship had been challenged by Ava's deceased husband's infidelity with Alani's daughter, Mia. The discovery of the relationship had devastated both families.

Even more crushing had been Alani's cancer diagnosis a few short months ago. After healing from a double-mastectomy, the doctor had finally determined that Alani was ready to start her chemotherapy regimen.

As warned, Alani grew terribly ill with the side effects. Ava made a point to visit every day.

Ava pulled into Alani's driveway and cut the engine.

Elta bent near a bedding area. With clippers in hand, he turned and greeted her.

"How is she today?" Ava asked, as she walked in his direction.

He slowly shook his head. "It's hour by hour. Right now? Good. She ate some poached eggs this morning and was able to keep them down. That's a good thing, right?" He looked at her, hopeful.

Elta stood and brushed off his jeans. "Ori was scheduled to take Mia to the airport this morning. She was going to take a short trip to retrieve some of her things, but I asked her to stay."

Ava closed the space between them and drew her friend's husband into a hug. "I know this is hard, but Alani won't always be suffering this much. The chemotherapy is the devil, but he's not going to win this one," Ava assured, as much for herself as the man in her arms.

When she released Elta, he wiped at his eyes with the back of his gloved hand. "Yes, God is good, and He's in control. The one who knows how many grains of sand are on that beach over there is the same one who already knows the number of my wife's days."

Ava nodded. "Healed, or heaven." She repeated Alani's often quoted phrase, and both she and Elta shared a chuckle.

"Yes. Either way, this story ends well," Elta said, his face brightening with a smile.

Inside, Ava found Mia dusting her mother's furniture.

Elta and Alani lived in a modest home decorated with items that showed Alani's love of the island. There were highly-polished wood floors and rattan sofas with plush cushions covered in a tropical print. Her rooms had pots of towering foliage tucked in the corners and mounted ceiling fans with paddles that resembled palm leaves.

Mia looked up when Ava entered. While things remained tense between them, and might always be, there was a definite look of gratitude in Alani's daughter's eyes. "She got a little tired after breakfast and nodded off. She's in her room."

Ava nodded and headed directly there. The door leading to her friend's bedroom was cracked open. Ava quietly slid it open and peeked inside.

Alani was sitting on the bed, leaning against a pile of pillows. A half-empty box of macadamia nut chocolates sat next to her. Alani quickly stuffed the chocolate she held into her mouth and chewed furiously.

"What's that?" Ava pointed.

"What's what?" her friend answered, not bothering to hide the tiny dribble of chocolate at the side of her lips.

"Are you supposed to eat that much sugar?" Ava demanded.

"Are you supposed to interrogate me with all that nonsense?" Alani countered. She stuffed another chocolate into her mouth. "I haven't been able to eat in days. I'm hungry."

Ava parked her hands on her hips. "Shouldn't you eat something a little more nutritious? Like broccoli, or perhaps some papayas or mangoes, maybe?"

Alani brushed off the suggestion with a wave of her pudgy hand. "Nonsense. I'm craving chocolate. Who knows how many days I have left on this earth? If I want chocolate, I'm eating chocolate." She closed the lid on the box and motioned for Ava to sit on the bed next to her.

"I'm having a good day," her friend reported.

"I heard that. Listen, I brought you something. I think you're going to be really happy."

Alani perked up. "What?"

Ava shook her head. "It's a surprise. Wait here."

Ava traipsed back out to her car and retrieved four small boxes. When she returned to Alani's room, she held out the stack. "I brought you some hair."

Alani's eyes widened. She leaned forward off the pillows to get a better look. "What do you mean?"

Ava felt like Santa Claus on Christmas morning. She placed the boxes on the bed and lifted one of the lids. Inside was tissue paper, which she carefully peeled back.

Ava lifted the contents and held up her surprise. "It's a wig." She grinned widely. "I brought you four. One is a bob. One is a short pixy cut. One is a cute beach wave." She paused and threw open another lid, lifting the contents. "And this one is long and a bit dramatic."

Alani gasped. "It's blonde!"

"Yes, I know that."

"But I'm native Hawaiian. Do you think I can pull that color off?"

Ava grinned. "It's all in the attitude, my friend." She motioned for Alani to lean closer. When she did, Ava gently pulled the scarf away.

Alani's hair was visibly thinning. Missing patches of her thick, black curls left skin showing through her scalp. Soon, her entire head of hair would all be in the bathroom trash receptacle, a victim of Alani's chemotherapy drugs.

"This is ridiculous!" Alani muttered as Ava gently fastened a velvet grip around her head and positioned the wig in place.

"There, take a look." Ava offered her a hand mirror from Alani's dresser.

Alani's eyes immediately filled with tears.

"Oh, honey...what's the matter?" Ava said, alarmed.

"It's...pretty. I guess I won't have to be bald after all."

Ava sighed with relief. "Of course, you won't." She quickly pulled the rest of the wigs from their boxes for her friend's inspection. "And, there's more where this came from," she promised.

Alani tilted the mirror and stared. "I look a little like Marilyn Monroe, don't you think? Only with long hair and a little heavier." She grinned.

Ava couldn't help it. Laughing, she pulled her best friend into a tight shoulder hug. "Yes, Alani. You look just like her."

4

Christel sat on her lanai, holding a bottle of beer in her hands, one that was growing warm. She wasn't sure why she even pulled it from the refrigerator. She'd quit drinking any alcohol once she and Evan decided to conceive.

Perhaps the gesture was an act of rebellion. Or of trying to return to normalcy.

It seemed the past couple of years had been marked by changes. Some good, like her marriage to Evan, but many had arrived on her doorstep highly unwelcome.

She'd lost her father, and her close friend, Mia.

And Jay.

Now, her family's business was teetering financially, and the feeling of security her position at Pali Maui provided was quickly fading. Pressure to right the listing ship was building. They all looked to her to salvage the profit margins...or so it seemed.

Yes, her mother shared that pressure. Even her other siblings felt the sting. Even so, she was the chief financial officer. She managed the cash flows, made the projections, and reported the impact of every monetary move they made.

It was a lot.

Add to that trying to get pregnant? Some days, she just needed to drown her sorrows in a bottle of beer.

Yet, even that was not an option.

Christel shook her head and rose, intending to pour out the tepid amber liquid and toss the bottle. Evan would be home soon, and she should put together a salad for dinner. Something topped with the fresh salmon her brother-in-law, Jon, had slipped into her hands as she got in her car to head home.

"Here, enjoy this. I'm worried about you, Christel. Maybe you and Evan should take a trip. Get away. All this will be here when you get home."

She'd politely thanked him while brushing off his suggestion. He didn't understand that she couldn't just pick up and escape this mess. Not when her family was counting on her.

As she turned to head inside, Evan appeared. He was still dressed in blue scrubs after having a heavy surgery line-up that day.

"Hi, honey," she greeted, then lightly brushed a kiss against his cheek.

Evan scowled and lifted the beer from her hand. "Christel, we discussed this. It's not a good idea to drink when...oh." His sentence drifted as the realization hit.

She wasn't pregnant.

Christel looked up into her husband's eyes and saw the disappointment. Her eyes pooled with tears. She hated herself for her weakness. A negative pregnancy test was nothing to cry over. They would try again. Next month the news would be better.

Evan's finger brushed the moisture from her cheek. "Ah, don't cry, sweetheart." He launched into a litany of encouragement that mirrored her self-talk. "We have lots of time. We'll just try again."

"Yes, I know. Next month," she managed.

She pulled away and headed for the door. Evan followed.

"You are simply under too much stress," he pointed out. "You need a break from all that is going on at Pali Maui."

Christel placed the beer bottle on the counter and opened the refrigerator door. "You sound like Jon."

When her husband lifted his eyebrows, she explained how her brother-in-law had suggested the same earlier. "It's not that I disagree. I do. It's not possible right now. Me walking out on this situation is akin to you leaving in the middle of a spinal fusion. It's not done unless you wish to cause further harm."

She reached for the romaine and tomatoes. "Will you fire up the grill? Jon gave us some salmon."

"Perhaps it's time for some medical intervention?" he suggested, gently.

Christel whipped around to face him. "What do you mean, medical intervention?"

Evan took the bottle she'd placed on the counter and emptied the contents into the sink. "Perhaps it's time for some tests...to make sure you're properly ovulating."

The notion irked her. "It's only been three months. I'm not certain that signals a problem with my ovaries."

He lifted the bottle from the counter and gave her a look filled with patience. "There might be a blockage in your fallopian tubes." He tossed the beer in the trash.

Christel scowled. "How do we know it might not be you?"

Another patient look. "Because Tess..."

Before he could finish, Christel angrily waved him off. She didn't need reminding his dead wife had done for him something she couldn't seem to be able to do. "Stop," she said, grabbing a salad bowl from the cupboard. "We'll try again. That's all." The tone in her voice left no room for argument.

Seeing the pain on her face, Evan backed off. He made his way over and pulled her into a hug. Leaning over, he kissed the top of her hair. "I love you, honey. It will happen," he assured. "And when it does, you'll make a wonderful mother."

5

Tom Strobe drove to Pali Maui, his truck bed loaded with lumber, paint, and a few landscaping supplies. Clean-up and rebuilding projects were slowly getting caught up after the storm, but the damage was still causing supply delays across the island, even after several months.

While much progress had been made at Pali Maui, Ava still had some minor projects around her own house that needed attention. Small things, like replacing a door frame that had been splintered by flying debris and an ornamental gate that remained down.

When he'd mentioned these things to her the other day, she waved them off. "That's the least of my worries."

That may be true, but he wanted to do something nice for her. Lift a little of the weight she carried on her shoulders.

He'd never met a woman like Ava Briscoe. Sure, she was beautiful. He loved how her dark brown hair framed her creamy skin and how the curls brushed her chin. He was mesmerized by the smoky eyelashes that fluttered ever so slightly when she was tickled about something...the depth in those hazel-colored eyes. Few women near his age had maintained their figure and still looked that good.

But her appearance wasn't what he found the most attractive. It was her determination. She fiercely protected her family and her precious Pali Maui. The storm's hit would fold many men to their knees.

Not Ava.

She didn't wring her hands and whine about the setback and the loss of her pineapple harvest. She didn't wallow in self-pity. Nor did she expect others to fix her predicament. Instead, Ava Briscoe plastered a decisive resolve inside her spirit and marched forward with granite purpose...to restore Pali Maui and save her children's heritage.

In her spare time, of which there was little, she extended help to her neighbors and church members and donated time and resources to Ka Hale a Ke Ola Resource Center. He'd even learned she climbed up on the roof of the Banana Patch to help secure plyboard over a hole to keep the rain from coming inside.

Rarely did she ask for help. Rarely did she believe she needed help.

Tom shook his head. Everyone needed help sometimes.

He was unloading his truck when Ava came out of her house. His heart raced a little at the sight of her.

"What's this?" she asked, surprised. She headed his way.

Tom unlatched the tailgate. "Snagged some supplies as they came in. Thought I'd help you out a bit."

"Oh, Tom. You didn't have to do that."

He gave her a warm smile. "I wanted to."

There it was again...the flutter in her eyelashes. His effort had made her happy. That made him happy.

She invited him in. "Well, I'll let you take on these projects with one proviso."

"What's that?" he asked, following her up the walkway.

She lifted a pair of gloves off the table in the front foyer and slid her hands inside. "I'm going to help you."

That made Tom chuckle. "Why doesn't that surprise me?"

They decided to tackle the gate first. It took several trips to unload his truck.

Tom inspected the broken boards, determining the extent of repairs needed. "Who knew some wind and rain could tear up things like that?" he said, brushing sawdust off his gloves.

After unscrewing the remaining single hinge that remained in place, Tom lifted the gate and leaned the structure against a nearby fence panel. Together, he and Ava removed the screws that held the broken pieces of wood in place.

"You're an expert at that," he noted, enjoying the smell of her hair as he reached across her for the replacement hinge.

She gave him a sly grin. "I've had practice."

Tom reached for his tape measure. "Excuse me for saying so, but most women—"

"What? You're surprised a woman knows how to wield a screwdriver?"

"No." He paused. "Well, maybe." He grinned. "You have to admit; it is a little unusual."

"Tom Strobe. Don't tell me you are a—what's the word they use these days? A misogynist? No, that's too strong. Chauvinist maybe. Are you a chauvinist?" She chuckled, daring him to answer.

He shrugged and tossed a broken piece of wood to the side. Grabbing for a new board, he gave her a pained look that was purposely exaggerated. "I don't like to think so. I mean, you running this entire operation is kind of...attractive."

He let the statement sit there, knowing she might not know what to do with his bold declaration.

The truth was, he'd spent a lot of time thinking about this woman lately. Even though Ava had captured his thoughts, it didn't mean anything would ever happen between them. Ava had complications. He had no idea what she was dealing with beyond the obvious financial stresses and her friend's illness, but that occasional sadness in her eyes came from out of the past. There was something she was trying to get over. Something far deeper than she'd ever disclosed.

That didn't stop him from drifting off to sleep at night, more aware than ever of the thundering silence, the empty spot beside him in the bed. What would it be like to have a woman in his life again? Would he ever risk it?

After the pain of his divorce, he vowed he would never go there again.

Enter Ava Briscoe.

She made him realize how foolish he was to think he wanted to live a life of solitude. Maybe he was too quick to vow off women.

Romantic relationships were not worth the trouble or the risk. Yet, lately, he'd begun to think a little differently.

Never say never.

AVA FELT the urge to shake her head to make sure she'd heard Tom correctly. Had he said he found her...attractive?

Her heart started involuntarily thumping inside her chest. She pulled off her gloves and wiped the sweat from her palms against her jeans and took a deep breath to settle herself.

No...it was entirely too soon. Too soon after losing Lincoln. Too soon after the discovery of his affair with Mia had stomped on her heart.

That was the worst thing about betrayal. It emptied you. It kept you from wanting to reengage and feel again. At least in the romance department.

If you did dare to imagine what might develop and how that would be, the emptiness deep inside her quickly reminded it was not wise to go there. Loving was a two-way street and her lane had been closed in the aftermath of Lincoln's death and betrayal.

Ava didn't look at Tom. "Are you thirsty? I'm going in for some lemonade."

She felt him smiling at her. "Yeah, sure. I'd love some."

She shoved the screwdriver into her back jeans pocket and wiped her brow with her forearm, promising to return quickly.

Without looking back, she carried Tom's image with her as she headed inside. Few men looked that good in a flannel shirt and jeans. Fewer men were as generous with their time or offered as much help as Tom Strobe. Frankly, the renovations would have taken much longer without his concerted attention. His contract delineated his responsibilities, but he'd purposely extended the scope of this work well beyond simple obligations.

Admittedly, it felt good to have a man of his caliber step up and voluntarily go shoulder-to-shoulder with her. She knew his time was in high demand. He was a busy man on multiple levels. She wouldn't be surprised if he had contracts stacked up on his desk waiting for his attention. Even so, he'd made the Pali Maui project his priority.

He'd made her his priority.

Not even Lincoln could boast that. In fact, just the opposite. The real work at Pali Maui had always fallen to her while Lincoln leaned toward marketing, declaring that was his strength. He wined and dined customers who visited the island. He threw parties for the hotels and restaurants that regularly ordered from them. He attended all the industry conferences and functions. "Pali Maui must be represented," he'd often claimed whenever she suggested some of it might be unnecessary.

Never had her deceased husband hired anyone, fired anyone, jumped through all the hoops required by the Department of Agriculture or the Maui Office of Environmental Management. Was it Lincoln who filled out the mountains of paperwork? Did Lincoln work with Christel to prepare the projections and the forecasts? Did Lincoln lose sleep when signs of root rot showed up in recently planted pineapple crowns?

Ava gritted her teeth. *Stop*, she told herself. Quit going there.

Letting herself fill with resentment and anger was a dangerous trek that led to dark valleys in her soul. And that was without adding Mia to the mix.

Dwelling on Lincoln's failings kept her from appreciating that Tom Strobe was clearly interested in her. It's as if each time she recalled the hurt over Lincoln, she cemented another brick on her emotional wall.

Maybe it was time she began to drop her bricks.

What would it be like to permit herself to enjoy Tom's attention? Maybe to give in to it a little?

She was a grown woman. A single woman.

Did she want to spend her future years alone? Did she want to go to sleep at night for the next decades with no arms around her?

Ava drew a deep breath as she pulled some glasses down from the cupboard and moved to the refrigerator.

Tom clearly thought highly of her. His sentiments suggested he considered her to be brave...a woman filled with confidence.

Could she risk letting him see that inside she was scared to death? Scared of being hurt again. Scared that she couldn't take the kind of emotional hit Lincoln had forced upon her.

If she was to move forward and open herself up to the possibility of a relationship with someone—even someone as wonderful as Tom—would she end up sorry?

Deep inside, a tiny voice warned that life couldn't be lived too carefully if she wanted to live fully.

Ava lifted her chin and carried the tray of drinks out to where Tom was now hammering the replacement boards into place on the gate.

Thwack. Thwack.

Each time he raised his muscled arm and let it drop with force, the motion sent tiny shivers down her spine.

Stop thinking like that, she told herself again.

She wasn't some school girl. She was a relatively recent widow. She was a mother of four grown children. She was a grandmother, for goodness sakes.

What was going on inside her head?

Was it possible she could love again? Or, at a minimum, experience extreme infatuation? At her age?

She shook her head.

Never say never.

6

Two hours later, the repairs were finished. With Tom's help, the gate was repaired, several plants and trees taken out by torrential rain had been replanted, a splintered door frame had been replaced and painted...he'd even cleaned the pool.

"I don't know how to thank you," Ava said as he packed up. "With all the damage across the island, the contractors are backed up and supplies scarce. I still can't believe you got your hands on wood."

His eyes twinkled. "I have my ways."

She followed him to his truck as he loaded his toolbox into the back. "The least I can do to repay all this is cook dinner for you." She noted his expression immediately brightened.

Ava drew a deep breath. She hoped she knew what she was doing. No doubt she was marching into uncharted territory. He was interested in her, she could tell. Instead of thwarting his attention, she was opening the door. Was that a mistake?

"I'd love to," he answered. He paused. "Can you cook? I mean, I'm starving, and if..."

Ava gave him a playful slap against the arm. "I guess you'll have to take your chances. It would be rude to back out now."

They walked inside, and Tom asked to wash up. She pointed to the downstairs guest bath. "Don't be one of those who refrain from using the hanging towels. That's what they're there for."

"Got it," he said, grinning.

Ava moved to the sink and squirted some soap into the palms of her hands. She nudged the faucet on with her wrist and let the running water wash away the last traces of paint from her hands.

She couldn't help but ask herself again...What was she doing?

Tom left the bathroom door open, and she could hear him at the sink. It was crazy how the notion of him sent that buzzy feeling through her stomach. She tried to shake off the idea that she was acting Willa's age.

It had been a very long time since she'd felt that tingle of excitement. Even if good sense warned against it, she couldn't seem to shut those feelings down. Every effort to stop thinking in that way only reminded how powerful attraction could be.

Still, she had to keep her wits about her. She didn't need to invite a situation she wasn't ready to handle.

But could it hurt to at least be good friends? They had so much in common and enjoyed each other's company. It would be a shame not to embrace their developing friendship. She didn't need to let things progress past that boundary.

She'd keep her tingles to herself. She was good at hiding what she was feeling inside.

He came out of the bathroom, buttoning the cuffs of his shirt. "So, what's on the menu?" he asked.

Ava pulled her eyes away from his cowboy boots. Few people on the island wore them, and they looked good...manly.

He followed the trail of her vision. "You like my boots? I got them in Dallas while working on a big TPG project. Tournament Players Club is a chain of public and private courses operated by the PGA Tour."

She nodded. "I do like your boots." She moved closer for a better look. "What are they made of?"

"These are Lucchese, made of hand-stitched cowhide and ostrich. Best you can buy. Or, darn near."

"So, you have expensive taste?"

"Not necessarily. I buy very little. But, when I do purchase something, I want quality."

Ava invited him to sit at the island bar while she prepared dinner.

"That would be a pass," he told her. "I'm helping."

Now it was her turn to laugh. "Why doesn't that surprise me?"

"So, I hope you like pasta. I thought I'd make some homemade ravioli." It had been ages since Ava had bothered with the work-intensive recipe. It was one of her favorites. "I have a great wine I've been dying to uncork. I think it'll pair great with my mushroom gorgonzola filling."

Tom rubbed his hands together. "Sounds delicious."

Ava moved across her kitchen and bent to a lower cupboard to retrieve her hand-cranked pasta maker, a gadget she'd purchased at Williams Sonoma while on a shopping trip with Alani. The machine was chrome-plated and clamped to the countertop. The flat rollers created thin pasta sheets, and the ravioli attachment made little pillows of joy.

"Ah, now that's how I like to cook," Tom told her, inspecting the pasta maker. "Kitchen machinery. Right up my alley."

That made Ava laugh as she assembled the ingredients for the pasta...flour, eggs, olive oil, and salt. She pulled a large ceramic bowl from the cupboard and grabbed a large spoon from the drawer left of her sink.

Tom leaned even closer. "I don't think I've ever seen this done."

"Well, watch close. You're about to see a master at work." She tossed him an apron and donned one herself.

"First, you pour out several cups of flour on the counter and then make a nest."

"A nest?"

"Yes." She showed him what she meant by scooping a center. She cracked the eggs and let the contents drop into that center. Then she added the oil and salt."

Ava grabbed a fork, highly aware of how close he stood. So close, she could smell a faint aroma of his cologne mixed with a manly scent of sweat from working out in the yard. The fragrance was musky and left her knees a little wobbly.

Ava mixed the ingredients, trying not to think about how long it had been since she'd had any physical connection to a man.

She drew a breath. "The key to this step is to be gentle and keep the flour walls intact."

Tom nodded.

Suddenly, Ava reminded herself she should offer Tom some wine. She could sure use a glass. She directed him to where she stored the corkscrew and watched as he twisted the instrument into the neck of the bottle she'd placed on the counter.

Pop!

"There," he said. He leaned and grabbed the wine glasses she'd set out and poured the deep berry-colored liquid into the stemmed glasses. He picked one up, swirled the wine, and examined the legs left from the liquid sliding down the glass. "I love a good cabernet," he remarked. He took a sip. "Oh, yeah. This is delicious."

He slid her glass across the counter in her direction.

Ava had started to work the ingredients together with her

hands, forming a shaggy ball of dough. When Tom noticed, he lifted the wine glass to her lips.

She took a sip and tried to breathe. He was so close; it was heady.

Shaking off the feeling and the warmth of the wine in her stomach, she looked up at him. "So, when does this helping begin?"

"What? Pouring the wine wasn't helpful?"

"Of course. But don't stop there." She pointed to the dough. "This requires kneading." She stepped aside and motioned for him to take over.

He took a long sip of his wine and set his glass aside. He unbuttoned his cuffs, rolled up his sleeves, and began to press the dough with the heels of his hands. "Like this?"

She nodded. "The dough should feel pretty dry, but stick with the effort. It might not feel like it's coming together, but the dough ball becomes cohesive and smooth after several minutes of kneading. If you think the dough seems to be dry, sprinkle your fingers with water and continue kneading. If the dough becomes too sticky, dust more flour onto the work surface."

Ava enjoyed watching the way he knit his brows in concentration. She also enjoyed his broad shoulders and his strong hands.

She looked away and sighed. Her self-imposed boundary was being sorely tested.

Ava lifted her chin and went for the pasta maker with renewed determination. She fastened it to the counter, then looked over at Tom and announced the dough was ready.

"Okay, that looks great. We need to cover it in plastic wrap and let it sit thirty minutes."

Tom turned the job over to her, and he washed his hands at the sink.

Finished, he took his wine glass, and together they headed

for the living room. Ava grabbed a remote and turned on some soft jazz.

"Ah, Miles Davis," he murmured with appreciation. "Rolling Stone magazine described him as "the most revered jazz trumpeter." I agree. Easily, Davis was one of the most important jazz musicians of the 20th century. Did you know he retired only to make a comeback on the scene in the eighties and enjoyed an entire successful second run on his popularity? It seemed college kids everywhere discovered his music."

Ava leaned back against the sofa and closed her eyes, letting the notes seep inside and take her to another place, a place that was carefree and romantic. "He's certainly one of my favorites."

After the song ended, she opened her eyes to find Tom staring at her. The intensity in his eyes made her feel stripped of her defenses, and she looked away. Seconds later, she dared to glance back, and he was still watching her.

Between his attention and the warmth of the wine, she was in dangerous territory. Her sudden desire left her weak-willed and vulnerable.

Ava glanced at her watch. "Well, it's time to make the ravioli." She jumped up from the sofa and beckoned Tom to follow her back to the kitchen...back to safety.

She busied herself by unwrapping the ball. Wielding her fancy marble rolling pin, she furiously rolled out the dough, this way and that. Back and forth...until the sheet of pasta dough was only an eighth inch thick.

Tom watched her. "Need some help?"

"Nope. Got it."

She set the rolling pin aside and maneuvered around him, careful not to let their hips touch as she slid by. She pulled mushrooms and the gorgonzola cheese from the refrigerator, emptied them into another bowl, and lightly stirred the mixture.

He continued to watch her.

"Here, it's time to roll out the pasta," she said, cutting the ball into four pieces. She demonstrated this by placing one of the quartered pieces of dough into the trough of the ravioli maker. She cranked the handle and watched as a sheet of pasta flowed from the opening at the front.

Satisfied, she draped the sheet onto a space on the counter dusted with flour, then turned to Tom. "Your turn."

He duplicated her effort and made three more sheets.

When he'd finished, together, they spooned tiny spaced portions of the filling of mushrooms and gorgonzola onto the dough. Ava lifted another sheet of dough over the top and handed him her ravioli stamp. "Use this tool to crimp the sides of the little squares."

He reached for the stamp. When he did, his skin brushed against hers.

Ava took another deep breath and grabbed a second stamp. Shoulder-to-shoulder, they worked on finishing the task.

She brushed the flour from her hands. "That's it. They're ready to boil." She pulled a pot, filled it with water, added a dash of olive oil, and set it on the stove to heat up. She refilled their wine glasses, and they talked, waiting for the water to boil. When the water was steaming and ready to go, she placed the ravioli in the water. Minutes later, she retrieved the little cooked pillows from the pot and let them drain.

"Is there a sauce?" Tom asked, fascinated by the process he was observing.

She grinned. "Oh, no. Only butter."

He slowly nodded. "Ah, butter. The sauce of kings."

When the raviolis were assembled and ready to eat, Ava took a fork and stabbed a sample. She lifted it to Tom's mouth for a taste test.

"Careful, it's hot," she warned.

He took hold of her wrist and helped guide her hand to his

mouth. He took a bite, letting his eyes roll back with appreciation.

"Is it good?"

Tom moaned. "Delicious," he muttered. A drizzle of butter escaped and ran down the side of his mouth.

Ava reached with her finger and wiped the rogue sauce from the corner of his lips.

Tom grabbed her wrist and placed a series of kisses along her finger.

She leaned into him, unable to deny it felt pretty good to be that close. She placed a hand on his chest. "I think we'd best set the table," she said, breathless.

He lifted her chin and looked into her eyes. Said nothing. Just stared, reluctant to move.

"We should eat," she murmured.

He remained silent, staring. The hunger in his eyes was loud.

He took her in his arms, gentlemanly, and he moved closer.

This was it. *The moment of decision,* Ava thought. The truth was, she knew what was coming, and she wanted it. She didn't want to turn away.

Tom smoothed the hair off her damp forehead. "I'm going to kiss you now."

What the heck, she thought, feeling light-headed and completely unable to resist. She lifted on her tippy toes and slid her lips over his with delicious intent.

This was the kind of guy who would put his business interests aside to focus on hers. This was a man who would help her rebuild, who would notice and repair the small things around her house that had gone neglected. This was a man she could talk to for hours, trading stories and sharing interests they had in common. She enjoyed his company.

It's okay to feel something besides hurt and betrayal.

Tom responded by kissing her back, deeply. "Oh, Ava," he

said hoarsely. "He went in for a second kiss, this time lingering. She felt his lips against her own, felt the warmth, and savored what she'd missed so very much...a man.

Her fingers went to his hair, and she stroked the back of his head as his lips continued to move against her own.

"Gram?"

Both Tom and Ava were startled. They pulled away, and Ava looked toward the voice...Willa's voice.

Her granddaughter was standing staring. Next to her stood Shane holding Carson.

7

"Oh, sure. It's okay for Gram to make out with some guy...but if I do, I'm toast."

Katie rolled her eyes at her daughter. "Your grandmother is a grown woman. There is no comparison, Willa."

Jon chuckled under his breath. "That's contrary to what you said earlier."

Katie looked at him with daggers. "You hush!" she warned, in a voice just above a whisper. "Or you might end up grounded as well."

Jon laughed and made a motion like he was zipping his mouth.

"I can hear you," Willa called out from the living room. "And no matter my age, you grounded me for nearly six weeks. That was overkill."

Jon quit whipping the bowl of eggs. "You drove our car without a license...and without asking. *That* was overkill."

Katie held up open palms. "Will you both just give me some peace? I'm trying to put together some numbers Christel wanted for the concerts." She checked her watch. "I have less than an hour before I have to meet her and the boys for lunch."

The truth was, Katie was distracted by far more than her family. Her mother was caught making out with Tom Strobe!

No matter how hard she tried, she couldn't wrap her mind around the fact that her mother was kissing someone other than her father. Oh, sure...her mom certainly deserved to move on. Katie wanted her to, at some point. Just not yet.

Katie needed time to wrap her mind around this new development. Whenever she had imagined her mother falling in love again, the images in her mind included gray hair and rocking chairs. Her aged mother clinging to the hand of some faceless octogenarian with purple veins on the back of his hand, his walker close by.

In her wildest dreams, she'd never conjured up Tom Strobe with his face planted against her mother's and them lip locked.

Jon's arms folded around her from behind. "Let it go," he whispered against her ear.

Katie turned. "How do you do that exactly? Know what I'm thinking? It's kind of creepy."

Her husband didn't answer. He simply turned her around and kissed her, a little longer than was necessary, given that their daughter was watching.

"Eww," Willa complained. "Get a room!"

IN THE CENTER OF PA'IA, and only a short distance from Christel's house, was Charley's, a popular bar and restaurant where graybeard bikers and young surfers both lined up for the best food and fun around. Willie Nelson claimed Charley's was his kind of place and often played impromptu concerts on the tiny stage anytime he visited the island.

The owner was a friend of their family's and a customer.

Pali Maui delivered cases of fresh pineapples every morning. Or they had, before the storm.

Christel was escorted to a corner booth at the rear of the bustling establishment, where her siblings were already seated.

"Goodness, what took you so long?" Katie complained as Christel slid in beside her.

"Traffic," Christel reported, taking in the delicious aroma of bacon frying. "There was a slight fender bender just outside of town, and wouldn't you know it; Web Green showed up." She turned to her sister. "I could still throttle you for secretly setting me up on that dating website. I've been married for months, but that doesn't keep Deputy Barney Fife from sauntering up to my window this morning and using all his moves."

Aiden laughed. "Oh, this sounds good."

Christel grabbed her napkin and placed it across her lap. "Yeah, if Web called me *babe* one more time this morning, I was going to reach out of the car window and grab his skinny neck."

Katie couldn't hold back her grin. "Does Evan know he has competition?"

Christel huffed. "Okay, move on. Let's talk about something else." She turned to Shane. "This is where you normally weigh in. Why so quiet?"

Shane rubbed at the back of his neck. "I'm forever traumatized. Seeing Mom sucking face with Tom Strobe scarred me forever."

Aiden busted out laughing. "Paybacks for all the times she opened the rear door of your car in the middle of the night to find you half-clothed with some gal."

"Ah, c'mon. Completely different scenario. This is Mom."

Even though she always ordered precisely the same thing, Christel grabbed a menu. "I'll have an omelet, hold the hash browns," she told the waitress. "Oh, and a glass of orange juice."

She turned to face her siblings. "Admittedly, I'm with

Shane. It's a bit unnerving to consider Mom romantically involved with someone."

Katie tossed her hands in the air. "Thank you. That's what I was telling Jon this morning. It's just weird."

Aiden unloaded a packet of sugar into his mug of coffee. "It was bound to happen sometime. Mom is an attractive woman, and she's not that old." He picked up a spoon and stirred. "Tom Strobe is a great guy. He seems to think a lot of her."

Shane folded his arms across his chest. "Well, it's not like we have any say in the matter. Paybacks or no—I hope I never have to witness the fruit of his attention toward her ever again." He shuddered.

Katie leaned and pulled some papers out of a bag nestled at her feet. "Here are the numbers you asked for."

Christel lifted the documents from her sister's hand. "What do they show?"

Shane piped in. "The numbers should look good. I lined up some of my buddies to play...for free."

Christel rolled her eyes. "We don't need any EDM. The real money will come from catering to a generation a little older than yours." She slipped through the papers, reviewing the figures Katie had put together. "Besides, we don't want to scare all the birds off with loud electronic banging pretending to be music."

Shane frowned. "No, nothing like that. I lined up Soul Kitchen. Normally, they charge well over a thousand dollars per event. They know that hit Pali Maui took in the storm, and they're offering a complimentary evening."

This caught Christel's attention. "You're kidding?"

Soul Kitchen was a trendy musician group on Maui known for their acoustic-infused music, which crossed genres of soul, blues, jazz, and a bit of island rock. The vocalists often delighted their patrons with four-part harmonies sung in an exotic, sweet style.

"I used to date one of the lead singers," Shane bragged. "She was more than happy to hook us up."

"Date?" Aiden teased. "You use that term loosely."

Shane reached and punched his brother's arm. "Well, you need to take off your monk's cape. When was the last time you even considered connecting with a girl? Outside holding a female in the water during a rescue, I mean."

Christel couldn't argue with Shane's assertion. She came to her older brother's defense anyway. "Aiden's love life is not on the agenda." She pointed to the performa. "These numbers are impressive. This idea is a good one."

Katie beamed.

"And yes, Katie. You get all the credit. Holding concerts at Pali Maui is an amazing concept."

The waitress appeared at the table with their food.

When everyone had their plates, Christel picked up the salt shaker and continued. "When can we start advertising?"

Katie grabbed her fork. "I'm planning the big kick-off two weeks from Friday. Jon is going to put box lunches together. We'll sell tickets online starting as soon as possible. Aiden helped me with the website. We're set to go."

Christel was impressed. She held up her juice glass. "Here's to Katie and her idea."

The others held up and clinked their glasses in a toast. "To Katie," they said in unison.

8

Ava retrieved the last of the grocery bags from the back of her SUV. Before turning for the sidewalk, she spotted a familiar car heading up the winding drive, going a little too fast...as always.

She stifled a groan and shut the hatch door with one hand while juggling the bag of food items with the other, then waited until her sister's car pulled up and cut the engine.

"Hey," Vanessa called out. "Thought I'd stop by for a quick minute before heading home."

Home was only a short walk away. Ava had lent one of the workers' shanties to her sister free of charge—until recently when she urged a monthly rent check. Ava's original offer was meant to help Vanessa get back on her feet financially after losing her anchor job at a top television station in Seattle. They'd not often seen eye-to-eye, but she was still family. Ava had a hard rule about turning away family when they were in need.

Sadly, Vanessa didn't seem to have that same mindset. She'd choose a pair of Christian Louboutin pumps over her blood relatives any day of the week. While Vanessa might argue differently, her idea of familial support was limited to getting identical tattoos with her nephew.

Even Vanessa's teenage daughter elected to live with her father and had very little to do with her mom, except an occasional one-word response to a text.

Ava shoved the bag of groceries into her sister's hand and bent to deadhead the hibiscus bush near the footpath that led to her front door. Vanessa didn't protest. Instead, she followed Ava inside like a puppy dog.

"So, what's up?" Ava asked. Something was always up with her sister.

Vanessa placed the bag on the kitchen counter and went for the refrigerator. She retrieved a can of La Croix and popped the top. She held up the can. "I'm sorry. You want one?"

Ava shook her head. "You didn't answer my question."

"What?"

Ava pulled a loaf of bread from the bag. "You don't casually stop over for a visit unless you want something."

Vanessa waved her off. "That's not true." She took a drink and looked at Ava over the top of the can. A grin formed.

"What?" Ava demanded.

"I heard Tom Strobe kissed you."

Ava grimaced for a second time. "Oh, you did, did you? Which of my kids spilled?"

Vanessa grinned. "None of them. It was Willa."

Ava placed the bread in the pantry and huffed. "Figures."

Vanessa kicked off her heels and leaned over the kitchen island. "So, it's true?"

Ava answered her sister's question with silence. She reached inside the bag, grabbed the container of milk, butter, and a carton of eggs, and headed for the refrigerator, juggling the items with skill.

"What? You're not going to tell me?"

"That's right. I'm not going to tell you." Ava placed the items on the refrigerator shelves and closed the door with her hip. "My private love life is just that...private."

Vanessa scowled. "But where's the fun in that?" She slid onto a barstool. "So, did he use his tongue?"

"Vanessa!"

Her sister held up open palms. "Okay, okay. Yikes. When did you get so sensitive? I think you've grown a bit grouchy with all this time on your hands lately."

"Time? Do you mean all that free time I have dealing with banks and loan documents and re-negotiating shipment delivery dates? I can go on but let's change the subject," Ava suggested as she continued putting away her groceries. "How are things in the campaign office?"

Vanessa grew a smug look on her face. "Well, I hate to say so myself, but I think Jim Kahele applauds his decision to bring me onto the team. Since joining the campaign, I've focused our messaging, created visual branding, and lined up speaking engagements and media tours. Poll numbers are soaring in our favor. No thanks to that mother of his, I might add. Did I tell you what happened with Lucille?"

Ava shook her head, grateful and not all that surprised that Vanessa had taken the bait and turned the topic onto herself. "No, do tell."

"Well, Axel...that's her cat...climbed up on Scott BeVier's desk and started biting his wrist while he was typing. Scott is on loan to us from the University of Nebraska as part of a political science intern program."

Ava grabbed herself a soda and motioned for Vanessa to follow her out to the lanai. "Her cat bit him?"

Vanessa nodded. "Oh, yes. Apparently, Axel hates the clicking noise the keyboard makes. Seems no one else's keyboard, just Scott's."

Ava motioned to two chaise lounges. "What did you do?"

Vanessa straightened her shoulders. "Every person in the

office, including Jim, is scared of that damn cat. Well, I'm not. I took hold of that thing by the neck and threw…"

Ava's eyes grew wide. "You threw Jim's mother's cat?"

"I did. Right onto the floor," Vanessa said triumphantly. "And if that mean feline tries it again, it will get locked in the bathroom."

"Oh, my goodness! What did Jim's mother say? I bet she threw a fit."

"She did. Lucille threatened to tell Jim and have me fired." Vanessa slid onto the chaise and lifted her face to the sun. "I told her to have at it."

Ava's eyebrows shot up in astonishment. "That was a brave move."

Vanessa laughed. "Kickback, our IT kid, stepped in the middle of things and calmed the 'ole bat down. He pulled the cat out from under the table and handed the nasty thing back into her arms—totally unharmed, I might add."

Vanessa's actions were incredulous to Ava. Personally, she would never have the nerve to openly offend someone—especially her boss' mother. That wasn't the only difference between Ava and her sister.

When it came to men, Vanessa was a player, often dating multiple men simultaneously. There were times she had two dates in one day and thought nothing of it.

On the other hand, Ava felt paralyzed every time she thought about how the line had been crossed with Tom Strobe. Once you go *there*, you can't go back.

Vanessa would say a kiss is just a kiss.

Not true. That kiss meant volumes.

What scared Ava the most was how her mind seemed to be taken over with thoughts of Tom. She went to sleep at night thinking about how he smelled. She woke and saw his eyes looking into hers. She brushed her teeth playing conversations in her head—ones they'd had and ones they might have.

Since they'd met, Ava had learned a lot about Tom, but she wanted to know more. Besides golf, what kind of hobbies and special interests did he have? What was his childhood like? His parents? What scared him? What worried him? What thrilled him?

She was consumed. It was as if she'd lost control of her very mind.

And that frightened her to the core.

"So," Vanessa said, bringing Ava's attention back to the conversation. "As I said, that cat ordeal wasn't even the worst. You want to know what it was?"

Ava nodded. "Yeah, what happened?"

A sly smile sprouted on her sister's face. "I'll tell you, but you first. Did Tom Strobe use tongue, or not?"

9

"I don't know why I let you talk me into this," Christel complained. "I should be at the office." She let her voice drift off.

Katie drummed her thumbs against the steering wheel as she searched for a parking spot. "What could be so pressing that you can't spend a little time helping me at the rental store?"

Katie had a point. Losing most of their harvest in the storm had interrupted her typical schedule and freed up time, so here she was in the car with her sister going shopping.

"You know I hate to shop," Christel pointed out as she reached for her purse.

Katie pulled into an open spot and cut the engine. "Well, Amazon doesn't deliver rental chairs. So, come on." She unbuckled her seat belt. "This will be fun."

They headed into the rental store with Katie babbling on about her plans for the upcoming concert. Her excitement at the potential for these events to raise funds for rebuilding Pali Maui seemed to be increasing by the minute.

Or, maybe it was simply Katie. She loved a new project.

According to Katie, the public relations firm their Aunt Vanessa enlisted had booked online advertising and set up an event with invites going to all residents in Maui. They had posters printed, again using discounts Vanessa had arranged. Shane and Aiden had rallied all their buddies and pasted the colorful advertisements in retail windows across the island.

The debut concert was scheduled for a week from this Saturday. As planned, Jon's restaurant staff would prepare box lunches to be included in the admission price, along with a lawn blanket with the Pali Maui logo. "Good branding is essential," Vanessa advised.

The most thrilling aspect, according to Katie, was that they had booked Medley Pacific, an energetic gypsy-jazz band with an island flair. The musical ensemble would be a huge draw and guarantee the event would be a success.

The rental store was nearly vacant. Katie looked around. Finding no one behind the counter, she headed for the cash register and dinged the bell on the counter. An older woman with gray hair lumbered into the room from behind a curtain. "Hold your horses. I'm coming."

Christel and Katie exchanged glances.

When the woman finally reached where they stood, Katie cleared her throat. "Hi, I'm Katie Ackerman. I called this morning."

"Yup," the woman replied. "Got 'yur chairs in the warehouse ready for delivery. All I need is the cash."

Katie looked at Christel.

Christel gave the older woman a weak smile. "Uh, could we see a contract first?"

The clerk cackled. "Contract? We ain't got no contract. Give us the money, and we'll give you the chairs. That's how it works." Despite the gruff response, her face sprouted into a toothless grin.

Christel opened her mouth to respond but didn't get the

opportunity before Katie spoke up. "That's good with us." Seeing Christel's immediate frown, Katie added, "We'll pay half up front and half upon delivery."

The old woman hesitated. "Well, I guess that would be acceptable." She smiled more widely now. "So long as you give me and my sister free tickets to this concert you're having." She raised one eyebrow waiting for an affirmative response.

Christel shrugged at Katie. "Your call."

Katie turned to the woman behind the counter. "It's a deal, so long as you agree to pick up the chairs by noon on the morning after the concert."

The old woman held out an ink-stained hand, and they shook.

Outside, Christel looked over at her sister. "You drive a hard bargain."

From the look on her face, Katie believed that to be a compliment. "Thanks."

Katie pointed in the direction of a department store. "Do you mind? I promised Willa I'd pick her up some new bras. That girl is going to end up better endowed than her mother."

Christel reluctantly agreed and followed her sister inside the department store as she headed for the lingerie section. Unfortunately, the route took them directly through the baby aisle.

Christel tried to avert her eyes without success. She couldn't help but admire the racks of tiny apparel in pastel colors.

"What?" Katie asked, noticing.

"Nothing."

Katie stopped and turned to face Christel. "Are you and Evan trying?" Without waiting for a response, Katie clapped her hands with joy. "You're trying!"

Christel grabbed her hands to silence the premature celebration. "Shhh...you don't have to broadcast your every thought."

Katie grinned back at her. "Are you...I mean, any luck?" She looked at Christel's midsection.

Christel waved her off. "No, not yet. I mean, we've had some disappointments."

Now it was Katie's turn to wave Christel off. "That's not uncommon. You'll try again and be pregnant before you know it." Her sister beamed. "I'm going to be an aunt again."

Christel wasn't so sure. Maybe she had waited too long and missed her window. "Well, there are no guarantees, but I hope so."

Katie refused to accept that negativity. "Oh, pooh." Her face broke into another excited grin. "You and Evan are going to have a baby!"

10

Ava had entirely too much time on her hands these days. Waiting for the emergency operation loan to come through so they could purchase the needed pineapple crowns from operations in Costa Rica seemed to be taking forever. Without those crowns, planting had come to a halt. With no harvest, shipping had come to a halt. With no mature fruit being waxed and boxed, local deliveries had come to a halt.

The only thing that hadn't come to a halt was incoming invoices. Bills still had to be paid. She and Christel had juggled what they could. The remaining expenses were placed in a pile until the next cash hit their bank accounts. Unfortunately, ripened pineapples had a short shelf life, and all their inventory had been shipped and paid for. The weeks ahead looked bleak unless that loan was executed quickly, and Pali Maui was in a long line of businesses seeking the same financial reprieve.

Ava tossed her now cold coffee in the sink, rinsed her mug, and placed it in the cupboard. She wandered into the den and made her way to her desk and home computer. She rarely sat and browsed the internet but thought she might take the opportunity to research some new organic chemicals coming on the market. The thick pineapple skins created a natural barrier to pests common in mangoes and other fruits, so that was of little worry. The new compounds reportedly increased growth...something Ava was now very much interested in.

She opened the internet browser and began typing...mistyping actually.

Before she could back up the curser, the word *chemo* appeared in the search window, and related articles filled her screen.

Ava swallowed. She couldn't seem to turn away as her thoughts moved to Alani and what her best friend was going through.

She clicked, and an article loaded. Ava grabbed her reading glasses and leaned forward to scour the information.

What she saw made her heart sink.

Doxorubicin , Alani's current chemo drug, was currently the most effective chemotherapeutic used to treat breast cancer. According to Elta, Alani's team had determined that using the "red devil," nicknamed for its reddish-orange color, was the best course of early treatment for Alani's aggressive breast cancer.

"The doctors report this is a war, and they want the best army battling on her behalf," Elta told her. He also told her the nurses had placed a pillowcase over the iv bag to hide the concoction as it drained into Alani's veins.

From this article, there were horrible side effects. Severe nausea and vomiting were at the top of the list. The drug often changed the appearance of a patient's skin, making it appear rusty in color. Some even experienced similar color changes in the white of their eyes. A high percentage of patients fought severe joint pain, fever and chills, and irregular heartbeat.

While most of these symptoms could be managed at home, there were times when the situation worsened to a level that required hospitalization, especially if the patient were to become dehydrated.

Ava sucked in a deep breath and closed down the computer.

She pushed back from the desk, grabbed her purse and keys, and headed for her car, not even bothering to put on lipstick.

Ava made her way to Wailea in record time. Thankfully, she passed no highway patrolmen. Upon arrival, she was blocked from pulling into Elta and Alani's driveway by a vehicle she didn't recognize. It wasn't Ori's. He'd recently traded in his old sedan for a more economical moped that was barely legal for the highway. As she walked past the car, she noticed a dashboard hula girl and shook her head. The owner was definitely not anyone she knew.

At the entrance, she pushed the doorbell and waited. The door immediately swung open, and Elta appeared. He looked a little harried.

"Hi, Elta. I should have called, but I thought I'd drive over and spend a little time with Alani. How is she today?"

Over his shoulder, she could hear a commotion. She raised on her toes for a closer look.

"Ladies from the church," he said, his voice low.

Ava's brows pulled into a puzzled frown. "From church?"

"They showed up to help with buckets, mops, brooms, and a lot of loud chatter," he bemoaned. "And they've been here all morning."

Ava gave him a sympathetic look and patted his shoulder. "The saints came marching in, huh?"

He nodded and whispered, "And then some." He raked his hand through the top of his jet-black hair before adding, "Don't get me wrong, their service is much appreciated. Especially since the time came for Mia to make a quick trip to the mainland to retrieve some of her things and make arrangements with her employer for an extended leave of absence." He shook his head. "These ladies are the feet of Christ walking out their faith," he remarked. "Goodness knows, I certainly don't relish scrubbing toilet bowls."

Elta stepped back, allowing Ava to enter. One of the women looked up and recognized her. "Oh, Ava." She dropped her sponge in the bucket and headed her way, enthusiastically chattering about how long it had been. Tried as she might, Ava didn't recognize the woman who pulled her into a tight hug as if they'd been friends for years.

As soon as the woman released her, she turned to her friends. "Girls, this is Ava Briscoe…from over at Pali Maui. She's the one I told you lost her husband last year." She turned back to face Ava. "That funeral was such a testament to the great man your husband was. A real tribute. Goodness, his loss was such a tragedy. Everybody on the island loved Lincoln, just loved him to pieces."

Suddenly, the name came to her. The woman standing there in her tropical print housedress, white sport-shoes, and ankle socks was Marilyn Eudaly. They'd met at the grand opening for the Banana Patch.

"Thank you, Marilyn," Ava replied. "I appreciate that."

She turned to Elta. "Mind if I go up?"

He nodded. "She's been asleep most of the morning." He looked at his watch. "But, she should be waking soon. It's time for her anti-nausea meds."

Ava quietly made her way to Alani's bedroom door and slowly pushed it open without knocking. She didn't want to wake her friend if she was still sleeping.

The bed was empty.

"Alani?" Ava called out, alarmed. Her eyes scoured the room for a trace of her friend.

That's when she heard what sounded like a wounded puppy. The sounds were coming from the adjoining bathroom.

Ava rushed for the door. Alani lay clutching a bath towel on the floor next to the toilet. She was silently weeping.

Ava dropped to her side. "Alani? Are you okay? What's the matter?" She yelled for Elta then turned back to her dear friend. "Oh, honey."

Her friend could barely lift her head. She squeezed her eyes tightly shut and reached for Ava's hand. "I need...I need a doctor."

AFTER AN EMERGENCY CALL TO 9-1-1, an ambulance transported Alani to Maui Memorial. Ava drove Elta, following closely behind the emergency vehicle.

In the subsequent hours, medical professionals consulted with Alani's oncology team. Multiple tests were run. Cardiovascular complications were quickly ruled out, and it was determined that Alani was severely dehydrated, which prompted uncontrollable nausea, fevers and sweats, and body aches. All these symptoms were remedied with IV fluid therapy. It was recommended that Alani remain in the hospital overnight so the medical staff could keep an eye on her progress before allowing her to return home.

Alani must have felt really ill because she didn't argue.

When she drifted off to sleep, Ava gently motioned to Elta. "C'mon, let's get you home."

"I'm not leaving her side," he argued.

"Elta, she's under the best of care. You won't be worth anything to her if you're next. You need to eat, sleep and be ready to come get her in the morning, fresh and able to be what she needs."

Reluctantly, he agreed.

In the parking lot, Ava and Elta slowly walked to the car. Elta was noticeably quiet.

He remained quiet as he climbed into the passenger side. Ava quietly sent up a prayer for him as she started the engine. He was going through hell, and he needed to have a touch of heaven right now.

As they pulled onto the highway from the parking lot, Ava gently mentioned he might want to call Ori and Mia.

Elta shook his head. "The children will only worry. I'll text them when I get home."

His shoulders sagged. Alani's illness and today's scare had taken a toll on her best friend's husband.

As pastor of Wailea Chapel, he had spent countless hours comforting others. As Ava had learned, wisdom disappeared when the situation became personal.

"I want nothing more, or less, than God's will in every situation...even this," he said, his voice slightly trembling. "But I pray He doesn't take my Alani home. Not yet."

Ava reached and covered Elta's hand with her own. Without uttering a word, she simply squeezed.

11

Tom Strobe climbed from his truck, painfully, and embarrassingly aware that his every waking moment was spent thinking about Ava Briscoe. From the moment he showed up at Pali Maui to discuss the golf course renovation, he was smitten. He wanted nothing more than to drop everything, sit down at a table, and get to know her.

After his divorce, he'd sworn off ever letting a woman get to him again. But Ava had an aura about her, something that got him all worked up.

He saw her nearly daily, often sharing meals and long conversations. She was becoming his closest friend, and he suspected he was quickly becoming important to her as well.

Ava was open about losing her mother at a young age and how she'd had to step up and become an adult far sooner than most girls. In her youth, she had shared a close relationship with her father, who was a doctor. He purchased Pali Maui and soon realized the acquisition created a mountain of responsibility he didn't have time for. As a result, Dr. Briscoe entrusted much of the day-to-day operation to Ava and pushed her into business very early while her sister enjoyed a carefree existence...a role she seemed to still embrace to a great degree.

Ava's greatest joy was her children and grandchildren. Anytime the conversation turned to any of them, her eyes lit up. He admired how available she seemed to be without becoming intrusive like some women he knew...the kind who tried to live their children's lives for them by offering constant unwarranted and uninvited advice.

She also loved Pali Maui. The hit the business had recently sustained nearly broke his heart for her. Yet, instead of wallowing in self-pity, she pushed hard to rebuild—despite financial strain.

Ava was brilliant and a force to be reckoned with...a true woman of substance. He admired her on so many levels.

Tom reached inside his truck, grabbed his clipboard from the seat, then shut the pickup door. He headed in the direction of what would soon become the new clubhouse, still thinking about Ava.

On the few occasions Tom had posed a question about her deceased husband, she quickly clammed up. While Ava remained closed-lipped about her marriage to Lincoln, Tom suspected it was a lonely union, at least from Ava's end. There were few framed photos of him in her house, and she rarely mentioned her dead husband, even though it had only been a little over a year since his passing.

It seemed Lincoln had abandoned her far earlier than the day he died. Whatever he'd done, he'd left her hurt and lonely.

Tom couldn't imagine any man, with half of his senses intact, not realizing how lucky he was to have a woman like Ava Briscoe. When she smiled, her whole face lit up. And when that smile was directed at him? Well, he hadn't known it was possible to melt.

He'd only taken a few steps when he saw Ava's car heading up the long drive. The sight immediately made him smile.

He slowed and watched as she approached and parked, intending to wave as she exited her car.

He waited.

Why was she just sitting there?

Concerned, he turned and headed her way. Upon approach, he knocked gently on the passenger window. That's when he noticed the tears.

He tucked the clipboard under one arm and opened the door. "Ava? You're crying."

She turned to him, looking shattered.

He dropped the clipboard and immediately bent and wrapped her into his arms. The position was awkward, but that didn't matter. Ava was hurting, and he wanted desperately to comfort her.

"It's Alani," she finally admitted.

Alarm instantly filled him. "Is she alright?"

Ava sniffed. "They kept her in the hospital." She told him about what had happened, how she had found her best friend on the bathroom floor. "She was dehydrated. Nothing that couldn't be reversed with some IV fluids, but..." She let her voice drift, and she choked up again. "It was so hard seeing her like that. Alani is the strongest woman I know. This cancer has leveled her. Completely leveled her. I can't lose her, Tom. I just can't."

Tom pulled her tightly against him. There were times when he knew to be quiet, simply be there...a shoulder to cry on. This was not one of them.

He took Ava by the shoulders and turned her to face him. Crouched in front of her next to the car door, Tom gave her a stern look. "Ava, stop. Breast cancer is not a death sentence. Alani has the best oncology team working on getting her through this." His eyes turned sympathetic. "I know losing your mother to the same disease makes it difficult for you to believe everything will turn out well, but you have to know that medicine has made incredible advancements. Alani is otherwise strong and healthy. We have every reason to hold onto the hope that she will someday look at this season in her rearview mirror."

He reached and wiped the moisture from her cheek with his finger, then lifted her chin to him. "You're not going to lose your friend."

"You can't promise that."

"No," he admitted. "But, come here a minute." He invited her out of the car.

She took his hand, allowing him to lift her from the seat. Tom picked up his clipboard and flipped the fastened pages until he landed on a schematic of the back nine. "See this?" He pointed.

She nodded.

"In a few short months, a golfer will be standing at that box. If he's an amateur, he'll try to get as much power as he can muster using his upper body and hit the ball as far as possible. Unfortunately, this would be a mistake."

Tom looked over at her. "The golf swing is a complex motion involving the whole body, not only the arms. Rarely does a golfer experience a hole-in-one. It often takes a sequence of successful drives, chips, and putts to par a hole."

He kissed the back of her hand. "I'm no doctor, but I hear medicine is similar. We can't expect Alani to get well overnight. No one thing will kick this cancer but a concatenation of complex procedures and medicines. There will be some days where Alani soars down the fairway and some that land her in the rough. Yet, I think we're all safe in knowing Alani's oncology team is not going to let her land in the sandbox."

Ava suddenly threw her head back and began to laugh. "You've got to be kidding, right? You didn't just compare my friend's health journey to a golf game, did you?"

He joined her with a chuckle of his own. "I may have."

She playfully slapped at his chest. "You are such a man!"

Ava might not have meant that as a compliment. Sure, his golf analogy was a bit lame, but that didn't matter to Tom. What mattered was the brightness in her eyes and the smile on her face.

He'd just been able to change her mood, give her hope and make her happy.

And that made him feel like he'd just won the Masters.

12

Katie wrapped the apron ties around her waist and gazed out her windows. In the distance, a small army of men assembled a stage platform with risers, sound gear, mic stands, and lighting. Beyond that, another group was busy putting up white tents and lines of chairs. The grassy area at the front would be reserved for attendees who had purchased premier tickets, which came with picnic blankets and box dinners.

Come dusk, a steady stream of vehicles would ease off the Kuihelani Highway through the iron gate leading to Pali Maui. To Katie's delight, her event had sold out, and, word had it, attending this outdoor concert was more widely anticipated than viewing a live volcano eruption on Haleakalā, the only active volcano on the island of Maui which last spewed lava over four hundred years ago.

Katie's phone dinged, alerting her to an incoming message. She pulled it up to find it was from Christel.

"Get down here. Workers are asking questions, and I have no idea what to tell them."

A smug grin formed on Katie's face as she relished the notion that, for once, Christel was not in charge. She was.

Her fingers furiously typed out a response. "Hold your britches. I'm coming."

Minutes later, she walked into the melee and was immediately accosted by a guy wearing a shirt embroidered with a company logo and carrying a clipboard. "Where would you like the flowers placed, Mrs. Ackerman?" Upon seeing the slightly confused look on her face, he instantly added, "Sorry. I'm Frank from Island Botanical. We're here with the flowers you ordered."

She pointed to four large urns positioned across the front of the stage. "There. You were able to get the blue passion flowers?" She held her breath, hoping for an affirmative answer. She had stretched the budget to include the rare blooms from Peru.

Frank grinned. "We did. Even better, we secured you a nice discount." He leaned closer and winked. "Appreciate the complimentary tickets for my wife and kids. No worries. I think you'll be happy with what we've got for you in the truck."

Katie was, indeed, not disappointed. The blue passion flowers contrasted nicely with the yellow and pink plumeria, the orange birds of paradise, and the spiky protea blossoms.

"Oh, honey. You've outdone yourself."

Katie turned to find her mother approaching. She was dressed in crisp white ankle pants. Her bright turquoise sandals matched a flowing linen tunic. Mother of pearl jewelry dangled on her wrists and ears. "I'm so proud of you, Katie."

She couldn't suppress her joy. "Oh, Mom. This has been the most fun I've ever had, even surpassing building our house. I was meant for this!"

Her mother pulled her into a shoulder hug. "Yes, I believe you were."

Jon waved as he approached from the direction of the restaurant. He was wiping his hands on a bar towel. "Babe, the boxes are nearly ready. Everything is coming together. It's just about showtime." He gave her an encouraging smile. "Your hard work is going to pay off, sweetheart."

Christel bounded up the sidewalk. "Yes, last I looked...we were raking in an amazing sum of money." She shoulder-bumped her sister. "'Bout time you showed up."

Katie drew a deep breath and savored the praise of her family. The concert was her brainchild, the work of her heart... and it sounded as though her event might pull Pali Maui out of the red, at least temporarily.

Her mom looked around. "Any sign of the boys?"

Christel pointed at the far parking lot. "Shane just pulled in. Earlier, Aiden texted that he was going with a skeleton crew at the station. He wanted to allow his team members to attend the concert. Apparently, that gal who sometimes gives him a hard time offered to stay behind and watch over things."

Katie let out a slight laugh. "That gal is named Meghan McCord. Ever since Aiden helped free her from the dangerous relationship with that Culvane fellow, well...I think there's a little fondness developing."

"You're suggesting Aiden has a thing for the girl from the station?" She shook her head. "You do know her arms are tattooed with tigers? Do you really think our straight-laced brother would be attracted to someone like..." She stopped talking and glanced around at her family's faces. "Oh, my goodness. You all agree?"

Ava patted her shoulder. "Oh, honey. Few of us control who we fall in love with."

Jon shaded his line of vision with a raised hand. "Speaking of...looks like Tom Strobe is here."

Ava's face instantly brightened. She waved off the grins on her daughters' faces. "Oh, stop."

Tom had spent most of yesterday and evening at Pali Maui directing logistics. To his credit, he had a knack for spotting issues before they became flaws in the physical accouterments needed for the event. This, coupled with his adoration for their mother, won him a special place in Christel and Katie's hearts.

They each hugged him.

"You look nice," Katie commented, stepping back to inspect his outfit. She whistled. "Nothing like yesterday."

He grinned. "Yeah, funny what a pair of golf shorts and a pressed Hawaiian print button-down, along with a little cologne, can do for a guy."

Ava folded into his embrace. "I ditto the sentiment."

Shane approached, carrying Carson. He had a diaper bag slung over his shoulder. "Hey, everybody," he said in greeting. "Wow, Katie. This is really corking."

Tom raised his eyebrows. "Corking?"

"Really fine, like uncorking vintage wine," Ava explained.

The skin wrinkled at the corner of Tom's eyes. "I guess I need to hang around young people more."

"Forget the kids. You need to hang around me more," Ava told him teasingly.

"Consider it done," he assured her with a wide smile. "My pleasure."

He took her hand, and the entire group made their way to the stage. Katie turned to Shane. "I can't tell you how much I appreciate you lining up Medley Pacific. I knew they would draw a huge crowd, but ticket sales far exceeded my wildest dreams."

Her younger brother shrugged. "Eh, they owed me."

Katie knew her brother spent time in late-night venues with friends who were musicians—or, at least, he had been before becoming a full-time dad—but she had never imagined the caliber of artists that were in his crowd. It appeared the same people who liked to surf and hang out were also the ones who were artistic and musically genius.

When Amy showed up with baby Carson, declaring Shane

to be the father, her younger brother had to grow up quick. Even more so when his girlfriend suddenly up and returned to the mainland, leaving Carson and only a note behind.

None of them would have estimated the extent of his responsibility. Since Amy left, he'd played sole parent, rarely depending on his family to help out except in emergencies.

He kept the house he'd purchased for him and Amy, paid utility bills on time, and took the trash out on the appointed day of the week. He grocery shopped and did laundry. In the middle of the night, he got up multiple times to give Carson his bottle and fell asleep burping him in the rocker.

To say the situation had put a severe crease in his social life was an understatement. Shane no longer stayed out all night, drinking and hooking up. He rarely spent the day at Black Rock, diving and hanging with his buddies.

He didn't surf, except on a few occasions when Aiden forced him to leave the baby with their mom. Didn't go to midnight dance parties on the beach. Didn't spend all his money on beer and corn nuts...or crazy tattoos.

No one saw this change coming. Not in a million years.

A loud whistle drew all their attention. When they looked in that direction, Aiden and Ori jogged to meet them.

"Hey," Shane said, fist-bumping his brother first, then their childhood friend. "What's up?"

Ava pulled from Tom's arm around her waist and tucked a stray lock of hair behind Ori's ears. "How's your mom today?"

"She's having a good day," he reported. "A couple of good days, actually."

Ava turned visibly relieved. "It's that good care she's getting from her family. You all have really been there for her."

"Mia never leaves her side unless she's forced to. She won't let Dad, or any of the church ladies, offer her a break. It's as if she—"

"Needs to pay penance?" Christel said, cutting him off. She instantly drew a breath. "Ori, I'm sorry. I—"

Katie cringed. Her sister's heart was in the right place, but her mouth often got a little misguided, especially when it came to Mia Kané.

Ori shook his head sadly. "Look, I understand. We all struggle with Mia's past. She's my sister, and I love her. Always will, but—" He let his voice drift.

"Of course, you love her," Ava declared. "We all love your sister." She glanced around, daring anyone to contradict her statement.

Katie could feel the tension building. While silent, Christel would never let go of what Mia had done to their family. She and Aiden struggled with it as well. Shane seemed to be the only one who didn't let Mia and their dad's affair bowl him over.

Yet, even he was puzzled by how their mother had so easily put aside the intense pain Mia had caused them all. One minute of consideration and Katie knew her mom had placed her feelings aside in consideration of Alani. Her best friend's cancer diagnosis had changed everything.

Tom frowned with confusion. "What am I missing here?"

Ava took his hand and squeezed. "I'm afraid that's a conversation better kept for another day."

13

By four o'clock, the party had barely started, and the lawns and chairs were already crowded. Ava wondered if the entire island of Maui had shown up. No wonder Christel was thrilled when she'd last looked at the sales figures. A big influx of cash would help liquidity and stave off the financial hardship they'd struggled with since the storm.

As Ava mingled, she happily spotted several people she knew.

Her brother, Jack, showed up over two hours ago with a leather bota bag slung over his shoulder. From the twinkle in his eye, she highly suspected his favorite whiskey was inside. Thor Magnum arrived with a tall, thin blonde at his side. He was the tattoo artist from Idaho who had designed the matching turtle tattoos on Vanessa and Shane. He's offered to do one for her several times. She'd politely declined.

Walt Bithell, their estate attorney, brought his entire family...which was large by anyone's measure. She lost count as twelve adults and as many kids piled from multiple vehicles.

Aiden's entire team from Maui Emergency Services filled

the first two rows of chairs. Workers from Jim Kahele's campaign office took up another row.

Willa's best friend, Kina Aka, and her mother, Halia, showed up with a large picnic basket filled with nutritious goodies. "Would you like an oatmeal cookie?" Halia offered as Ava leaned for a closer look. "One of the girls at the Banana Patch made them...with breast milk."

Ava tried not to visibly react. "Uh, no, thank you. They look delicious, though."

One person Ava hadn't spotted in a long while was Mig. She turned to Jon as he supervised another delivery of box dinners to the entry gate. "Have you seen, Mig?" she asked, helping him stack the boxes on the linen tablecloth.

Jon shook his head. "Nope. But if you spot Wimberly Ann, Mig should be close by. He's a besotted puppy dog whenever that woman is around."

Speaking of puppy dogs, Willa strode up with Givey on a bright yellow leash. She held her little sister's hand as little Noelle toddled beside her. "Hi, Gram. Hi, Dad. Have either of you seen Mom?"

"Your mother's running around like a chicken with its head cut off," Jon reported. "I highly suggest you don't bother her."

Willa's face screwed into a look of disgust. "Ew. A headless chicken paints a nice picture." She lifted the leash and her little sister's hand. "I don't want to play babysitter all night."

Jon looked at her with impatience. "Look, Willa... you'll have to buck up for a bit. We're all swamped. Won't hurt you to help out for a while."

"Help out doing what?" Shane asked, appearing next to them.

Willa laid out her long list of complaints—the fact that her friends were off having fun while she was tied down watching the dog and her sister was near the top.

Shane took pity on his niece. "I'll take 'em." He reached for the leash, then looked at Jon. "That okay with you?"

Jon nodded. "Yeah, that's fine. But you, little ma'am, you need to check in occasionally. And you'd best be thanking your uncle."

She jumped up and down and planted a kiss on Shane's cheek. "Thanks!"

Two seconds later, she was gone.

Jon gathered the empty crates and turned for the path leading back to the restaurant. "You sure you're okay with this?"

Shane gave him a nod. "You bet. No trouble at all."

Ava followed Jon and Shane, occasionally stopping to greet guests. When her son finally arrived at a vacant spot on the grass, he turned. "Mom, help a guy out?" He handed off the baby before spreading his blanket. Once he was settled, Ava placed Carson in the pop-up playpen.

"I'll be back," she told him. "I need to find Katie and see if she needs help. Then I'm going to find Tom. Last I saw him; he was helping troubleshoot the sound system."

Ava made her way to the stage area, taking in the noisy crowd as she passed, their faces filled with anticipation—the hint of sunscreen mixed with the aroma of lobster rolls and freshly-baked coconut cake wafting in the air as attendees opened their box dinners.

She couldn't help but wonder what Lincoln might think of it all. An event like this would be his crowning glory; she knew that.

SHANE PUSHED his shades up into his hair before digging in his diaper bag. "You want some snack crackers?" he asked Noelle.

She nodded enthusiastically. "Uh, huh. I want some trackers."

Shane opened and handed her a little bag. "There you go, sweetheart."

With the kids settled and Givey sitting next to him on the blanket, Shane surveyed the sight before him, not sure he'd ever seen this many people at Pali Maui at one time.

The event seemed to be a success. He was glad. It was hard seeing his mom and Christel so stressed out after the storm wiped out the harvest. Mentally, he chastised himself for not taking on more to help them. Sure, his hands were full. He didn't even remember when he'd last slept an entire night and not had to get up to care for Carson. Still, Pali Maui was his legacy too. The Briscoe family and Pali Maui were synonymous. Someday, the pineapple plantation would pass down to Carson, Willa, and Noelle.

There was a lot at stake, and he'd been extremely pleased to play a small part in helping put the concert event together by lining up free music.

Shane had known the guys with Medley Pacific for some time. They often hung out in the same crowd. The lead singer won several amateur surfing contests each year. The drummer could throw together a bomb party on the beach and introduced him to his famous crapper—a cocktail made with rum and pina colada mix and served in a toilet bowl with a floating chocolate bar. Party attendees simply took turns scooping a glass and drinking up until it became difficult to walk.

Boy, it'd been a while since he'd pulled one of those all-nighters with the guys.

Carson smiled back at him from inside the playpen, drool at the corner of his mouth, reminding him the sacrifice had been worth it. Still, if he were honest, he missed his old life.

"Hey, is this spot taken?"

Shane looked up and could barely breathe. A tall girl with long red hair cascading over her shoulders smiled at him. On a scale of one to ten, this chick was a thirteen. She wore a tight black tank top with shoulder straps that offered a nice view of her generous assets. Her cut-off jeans were frayed several inches at the hemline and barely covered her tiny round butt. Her legs were long...oh, so long. She was barefoot, and her toes were painted a bright pink. And she smelled like strawberries and syrup.

Shane stared for several seconds.

"So, is it? Can I sit?"

Her voice pulled him out of his trance. "Uh, sure. Yeah...lots of room." He motioned for her to join him.

She folded to the ground and helped herself to a drink from his cooler. "I'm Lindsay," she announced.

He swallowed. "Shane."

The sun goddess pointed to the kids. "And?"

"My niece and my kid," he explained, holding his breath. That wasn't usually a great pickup line. Likely, Lindsay would get up and tell him it was nice meeting him and be gone before he could blink twice.

She didn't.

"Cute." She sipped the drink. "You live nearby?"

"Uh, yeah. Pali Maui belongs to my family."

"Get out!" Her eyes went wide. "Your family owns this place?"

He nodded, now wishing he'd kept that piece of information to himself. He didn't need to muddy the situation with undue admiration.

"I mean, how rad is that?" she asked, clearly more than impressed.

Noelle tugged on his arm. "Potty. Me have to go potty."

Shane groaned. Not now!

He looked around and spotted Willa with her friend, Kina. He quickly waved them over. When he failed to get his niece's attention, he placed his fingers inside his mouth and whistled. "Willa!" he called out.

She turned and reluctantly headed his way.

"Look, your little sister needs to potty. Can you take her?"

Willa glanced at the girl on the blanket. Her face drew into an instant grin. She winked. "Uh, sure." She reached out for Noelle's hand. "C'mon, let's go."

Shane watched as they headed for a line of light blue porta-potty structures several yards away, on the other side of the parking area.

He turned back to Lindsay, meeting her eyes. "So, what brings you to the concert? Are you alone?"

She scooped some frosting from the coconut cake in Shane's lunch box and placed it inside her mouth, slowly drawing her finger from between her lips. "I'm on Maui with friends. We're on break from school...Yale."

Shane lifted his eyebrows. A knock-out and brains too. "Yeah? So, how do you like the island so far?"

"It was adequate...until a few minutes ago." Her implication did not go unnoticed. Neither did the spattering of playful freckles across her nose.

This girl was on the prowl. It'd been a long time since Shane had spent time with a chick this pretty, and he fully intended to take advantage of the situation. He'd pay Willa and her friend each a hundred bucks to babysit if he had to...but he would find a way to spend time with this girl.

The thought no more than left his head when he heard his name called out.

"Uncle Shane! Come quick! It's Noelle."

Shane could see the panicked look on Willa's face as she motioned for him to follow. Without thought, he scooped Carson from the playpen. "Where's your little sister?" he demanded.

Willa's eyes filled with tears. "She locked herself in the porta-potty!"

"You let her go in alone?" He shook her head. "By herself?"

Willa was crying now. "I thought she would be fine."

They raced to the line of porta-potties. Carson began to cry as he was jostled against Shane's hip.

Kina stood in front of a closed-door on a porta-potty third from the left. "She's crying."

Shane passed Carson into her arms, then bent and leaned close to the blue plastic door. "Noelle, honey? It's Uncle Shane. Don't cry. I will need you to be a really big girl, okay?"

He could hear her sniffles. "Noelle? Can you hear me?"

"I—I want out," she mumbled between sniffles. "I *tan't* get out."

"Listen, we're going to get you out of there. You have to follow and do what Uncle Shane tells you...okay?"

Without waiting for her response, Shane continued, "See that handle, sweetheart? Can you pull it down?" He eyed the tiny window with the word 'occupied' outside the door. "Noelle, take hold of the handle and push down."

"I *tan't* reach it."

Willa parked her hands on her hips. "That's not true, Noelle. You clearly locked the thing, so you can reach it."

This made Noelle cry again.

Shane turned to Willa. "Not helpful."

She shrugged. "Well, it's true."

Over the following minutes, Shane conjoled his little niece into trying to lift the lock. When he was unsuccessful, he finally turned to Willa. "You'd better go get your dad."

"Are you sure? He's going to be ticked."

Shane let out a frustrated sigh. "Go get your dad," he repeated.

"I'll go with you," Kina said.

"No, you stay here and hold Carson," Shane told her.

Minutes later, Jon ran across the parking lot toward them. Katie followed close behind.

"What is going on?" his sister demanded. "I leave you with Noelle, and this happens?"

Jon placed his hand on his wife's arm. "Stop; we don't know the circumstances."

Shane glared at Willa until she finally confessed. "I took her to the bathroom, and she locked herself in."

Katie charged for the locked door and leaned her head against it. "By herself? She could have fallen in!"

"Noelle, honey? Mommy's here."

"Hi, Mommy." The little voice seemed much chipper than moments before. "I locked in."

"Yes, I know, honey. We're going to get you out."

Both Jon and Katie tried to guide their young daughter to unlock the door from the inside, all to no avail.

Katie grew panicked. "Jon, what are we going to do? She's been in there a long time. It's hot…and she's scared."

"I'm not sure of that," he remarked. "The scared part, I mean."

On the other side of the door, Noelle was now singing. "Here comes Peter Cottontail, hopping down the bunny trail…" She belted out the song, now oblivious to her predicament.

Shane took Carson from Kina's arms. "Why don't you go get my mom," he suggested. "And Tom Strobe, if you can find him."

It wasn't long before Ava and Tom joined them. Ava added her concern to the situation. "How will we get her out of there?" she asked Tom.

"Wait here," Tom said. He headed off for his truck and returned with a small toolbox. He placed the oblong red container on the ground and lifted the lid. Inside, he retrieved a screwdriver. "This should do the trick," he told them.

Minutes later, the door fell off the hinges and onto the ground, revealing Noelle sitting on the floor of the porta-potty playing with a pile of toilet paper.

"Noelle!" Katie cried as she rushed to scoop up her tiny daughter. "Are you okay?"

"Me couldn't get out."

Katie smothered the top of Noelle's head with kisses. Jon turned and shook Tom's hand. "Thank you. I mean, really."

Tom shrugged and put his screwdriver back in the toolbox. "No problem."

Ava wrapped her arms around Katie in a big hug that encompassed her little granddaughter. "I'm so glad that's over."

In the background, Medley Pacific had taken the stage, and the entire crowd was clapping and swaying to the rhythm of the song they were playing. In the distance, the sun was slowly sinking into the ocean. The birds were no longer chirping, as if they, too, wanted to take a minute to enjoy the music.

Shane lifted on his toes and searched the place on the lawn where he'd left Lindsay in a rush. She was no longer there.

He sighed and placed his arm around his mother's waist. Just as well. That girl looked like trouble. As much fun as trouble was, it was…well, trouble.

They all walked back to the stage area together.

Except for the minor family drama, the evening was on track to be a huge success. Guests gathered for the debut outdoor concert at Pali Maui seemed to be having a good time. The gift shop was packed with buyers with a line of people wrapping outside the door waiting to get in.

Jon later told them the restaurant reservations had returned to a waiting list-only situation. Christel happily reported that their cash flow situation had much improved. No longer were their finances in the danger zone.

Katie's brainchild had saved the day!

The concert event was the first but definitely would not be the last.

14

Ava pulled on her rubber boots and headed out of her office walking in the direction of the southern fields where Mig and his crew were busy planting. The influx of money from the concert had allowed them to pay cash for a massive shipment of pineapple crowns from Costa Rica to replace what the feral pigs had eaten. They were back in business.

A warm breeze caught the edge of Ava's shirt as she made the short trek. When she reached her destination, Mig was nowhere to be found. "Hey, Kaleo. Do you know where Mig is?"

He pointed back at the office compound. "He called and said he was running a little late."

Ava nodded. Even her hard-working operations manager deserved a personal life that could intrude into work hours occasionally. Besides, he might have been up late taking part in post-concert fun.

She surveyed the landscape with a huge smile. There were pineapples in the redbud stage, more acres in high cone, while the lower fields, which the intruding feral pigs had not destroyed, were nearing harvest and boasting rows of nearly fully-grown fruit.

It took time, knowledge, and patience to grow a pineapple crop. Much of the process could not be automated and had to be done by hand. Pineapples grew best in sandy, loamy soil, which was plentiful here at Pali Maui. The pineapples were planted primarily from crowns, suckers, and slips—all variations of prior plants used to regenerate a crop. A skilled worker could plant up to five thousand new plants a day. Fourteen to seventeen acres were typically planted each week with fifteen to eighteen months for the fruit to mature for harvest.

Ava had overseen this process for years, yet she never quit being fascinated by the intricate process or the skill the workers used in their efforts.

A loud whistle drew her attention. She turned to see Mig heading her way, riding on his UTV.

"Ah, Miss Ava. Sorry, I'm late," he said as he cut the engine and climbed off.

She quickly waved him off. "You don't punch a time card around here. You know that."

Mig adjusted his cap. "Ah, yes. I know. But I like to be out here to ensure everything is going well."

"By the way," he said. "Last night's concert was an amazing thing."

Ava grinned. "It was, wasn't it? I never saw you, though."

"Ah, I got roped into some dancing. My Wimberly Ann barely allows me to rest for a minute."

Ava grinned at him. "You seem to be getting close?"

Mig sighed. "Ah, yes."

"But?"

"But, I haven't told Leilani."

Ava was shocked. "You haven't mentioned your new relationship to your daughter?"

Leilana lived in Honolulu. She ran a publicity company for

authors and was extremely busy. Mig bragged she had landed a big-selling romance author who lived in Seattle...a real career coup. Consequently, his daughter's schedule was so packed that she rarely made visits home.

Mig shrugged. "I kept meaning to, but every time I opened my mouth to say something to her over the phone, I felt like I was chewing on coconut shavings. Know what I mean?"

He paused and gave her a meaningful look. "Now it's too late. She texted last night that she is arriving today." He checked his watch. "Her plane should touch down any minute. I was late because I had to remove any traces of Wimberly Ann from my place. At least until I break the news to Leilani."

Ava offered Mig her sympathy. Juggling life with the expectations of adult children could be tricky. Goodness knows, she'd felt angst over her budding relationship with Tom and how that might play out with her kids...and grandchildren.

She patted her reliable operations manager on the shoulder. "You worry too much." She gave him an encouraging smile, wondering if that assessment was accurate.

Mig's daughter was known for being a bit high-strung. As a girl, she would have a complete meltdown if her socks didn't match her dress or if she got a B on a test and not an A. She quit eating dairy or meat at age thirteen, declaring she was officially a vegan. Sugar was akin to poison, according to Leilana Nakamoa.

Mig's daughter saw everything in black and white, no shades in between.

"Look, why don't you knock off this morning? We've got things well under control. You go pick up your daughter and take her to breakfast. It'll give you the chance to talk."

Mig's face broke into a grateful smile. Usually, he would never take her up on a proposition to leave his responsibilities behind. Yet, this morning, he saw the wisdom in her offer.

"Okay, yes. That might be a good idea." He squeezed her hand. "I'll be back to check on things soon after lunchtime."

Ava waved him on. "Go...everything here is fine."

He gave her another grateful smile, climbed on his UTV, and started the engine. With a wave, he was gone.

MIG NAKAMOA PULLED into the airport parking garage and drove, slowly ascending to the top floor where there were still many empty spaces. The last thing he wanted was to park his prized '55 Chevy Bel Air where some thoughtless fool would fling their door open and nick his shiny red and white paint job.

He cut the engine and sat for a moment listening to the last strains of one of his favorite Beach Boys tunes, Good Vibrations. The song filled his soul with memories of the summer he met Leilani's mother. That was a long time ago when he'd been a young man filled with dreams and hopes—a guy who could look the other way when the girl he'd fallen head-over-heels with had a mouth as sharp as any knife. He'd had to work overtime to please her and keep her from fussing. Ultimately, he'd lost that battle and she left him for another man.

Despite the pain of her abandonment, Mig wasn't sorry. Not when his former wife left him his sweet daughter, the treasure of his heart. Leilani gave his life meaning when he was lower than a rain barrel in a drought. Sure, she had a few of her mother's same tendencies, but he'd worked hard to guide her and teach her empathy and respect. More than once, he'd had to discipline the little girl. Each time, the punishment hurt him far more than it had Leilani.

Now, here she was...all grown up.

His daughter was beautiful, intelligent and very successful. He was so stinking proud of her accomplishments. She'd graduated summa cum laude from the University of Hawaii, gaining a double degree in Communications Arts and Creative Media. She was a marketing genius...at least that's what the online article said when she opened her public relations firm at the age of twenty-six.

At age thirty, she was well on her way to the top, reportedly one of the most up-and-coming female business owners in Hawaii.

Inside the terminal, Mig waved to the security guard, who was an old friend. "Hey, Nalu."

"Mig! Good seeing you, buddy. You taking a trip?"

"Nah, I'm here to pick up Leilani."

The older man pulled his uniform hat from his head and swiped his forearm across his face. "Well, I thought that looked like your daughter. She just headed for the rental car booth." He pointed.

"Thanks, Nalu." Mig patted his chum on the back and then raced for the tram that took passengers to where they could rent cars. Leilani was just about to board.

"Leilani," Mig called out. "Sweetheart."

His daughter turned. Upon spotting him, she lifted the overnight case located at her feet and placed the strap on her shoulder.

He hurried to her side. "Did you think your makuakāne would not pick you up?" He drew her into a hug, squeezed, then stepped back to get a good look. "Ah, Leilani...you are so beautiful."

She looked embarrassed as she handed him her bag and followed him to the parking garage. "You didn't need to take time off work and come. I was fully capable of renting a car."

He waved her off. "Nonsense." He opened the passenger door for her and placed her bag in the back seat. "How long can you stay?"

"Unfortunately, only overnight. I'm meeting with an author

at Oprah's compound tomorrow, and then I have to fly home for more meetings with some Amazon reps."

Mig was disappointed, but not surprised. His girl was known for burning candles at both ends...and in the middle.

On the way to Pali Maui, he told her all about Pali Maui... the storm that had threatened the operation financially and all that the Briscoes had done to stay afloat. He happily chattered on about the concert and the capital it had raised. He updated her on each of the Briscoes, Christel's marriage, and Katie's new house. Aiden had become captain at Maui Emergency Services upon the retirement of Captain Dennis, and Shane was a father of an adorable baby boy named Carson.

"Dad, you've told me most of this," Leilani reminded him. "Except for the concert. I'm glad it was such a success."

Mig's face grew a little warm. Yes, he probably had updated her. He clearly remembered that she sent Christel and Evan a lovely wedding present...a painting of the spot in Honolulu where they'd said their vows. He'd considered it such a thoughtful gesture.

Mig sighed. There was no mistaking that coconut shavings were again building in his throat. They were nearly to the turnoff to the lane leading to Pali Maui, and he had yet to mention Wimberly Ann.

He opened his mouth, hoping some words would come out.

Her phone rang. She immediately dug it from her bag and lifted the device to her ear. "Hello? Oh, yes. Uh, huh. We've moved the meeting back to Wednesday of next week. We have photographers from Publisher's Weekly meeting with us to do the photoshoot I promised." She tucked her head back against the white leather rest and let out a pleased laugh. "Yes, I assured you. You had no reason to worry."

Mig swallowed and geared down, preparing to make the turn. Clearly, it was too late to spill the beans now. He'd have to take Leilani to dinner, perhaps at her favorite seaside restaurant, Mama's House. Getting reservations at the last minute would be impossible, but he'd call and do his best. Word had it, Jon often bent his seating schedule around to accommodate the owners of Mama's House. It wouldn't hurt to hope for some reciprocation. He'd ask Jon to call on his behalf. That would cement the deal.

Immediately, he felt the stress leave his shoulders. Telling Leilani over a cocktail and hazelnut-crusted mahi-mahi was just the ticket.

Suddenly, everything changed.

There, parked right smack dab in front of his shanty, was Wimberly Ann's car. She stood beside the vehicle wearing a tight-fitted pair of white slacks and a red and white polka-dotted top with ruffled sleeves. The neckline was cut low. Matching red earrings dangled from her blonde hair that was fastened up on top of her head. Her lips were the color of cherries, as were the open-toed heels on her feet.

Wimberly Ann waved wildly in their direction.

Leilani shut down her phone and shoved it into her bag, leaning forward for a better look. "For the love of propriety, who is that?"

Mig swallowed the panic rising in his throat. He let out a cough.

"That's Wimberly Ann Jenkins. My girlfriend."

15

As soon as the door closed behind Wimberly Ann, Leilani peeked out the window, watching her head for her car. Seconds later, she turned. "Papa, have you gone completely lolo?"

Mig ran his hand through his thick black hair, tinged with gray. "What do you mean?"

Leilani parked her hands on her hips. "That woman is a... The fabric on her blouse barely conceals her, well...her woman parts." She squinted at him. "When I was in the bathroom, I texted my assistant and asked her to do a little research. Did you know she's been married six times?" Her finger jabbed the air in his direction. "Papa, you are not going to be number seven!"

Mig frowned. "Calm down, Leilani. Wimberly Ann is a sweet person."

"Sweet, my derriere. Just because she calls you Sugar doesn't mean her intentions are all chocolate and bonbons. Papa, use your brains."

Mig took a deep breath and headed for the refrigerator. "Do you want something to drink?"

"No, I don't want anything to drink! I want to understand why you have left all your good senses at the door and are seeing this person."

Mig let his daughter blow off her steam, knowing it was the only way she would ever calm down. He plucked the top off a cold beer despite her declination and handed it to her.

Glaring, she took the bottle and lifted it to her lips.

Mig also took several gulps from his beer. Dealing with his daughter when she got like this always demanded much patience.

These encounters were reminiscent of exchanges he had with her mother before she packed her bags for good. Sometimes, if things really got heated, his ex-wife even threw things. They never had a complete set of dishes because of her tantrums.

When several minutes had passed, Mig took a deep breath, hoping Leilani had settled down a little. "How is work? Tell me all about that new big author you are working with."

She placed the nearly empty beer bottle on the table. "Don't change the subject."

"I'm not," he said, clearly feeling the coconut shavings in his throat again.

His daughter challenged his assertion by raising her eyebrows.

"Okay, maybe I am," he admitted. "It's just that I hate seeing you get yourself so worked up over Wimberly Ann. You don't even know her."

"I know enough." She leaned her elbows on her knees and looked him in the eyes. "Papa, that woman is too flashy. She has a history with men...lots of men. She lacks class. Papa, she's just not right for you."

"You're wrong, Leilani," Mig argued. "She's kind and generous. Wimberly Ann is funny and wholly devoted to me. We have a lot in common and enjoy spending time together.

Please...try to get to know her before passing judgment. A person is not simply what they appear on the outside."

Her eyes narrowed. "You do not have a great track record picking out women," she reminded.

"I loved your mother. Yes, she was...difficult. The relationship was toxic and hurtful in the end. That doesn't mean that she's a bad woman."

"She's a horrid woman!" Leilani nearly screamed. "How could any woman leave her husband and baby and never see them again?"

Ah, there it was—the hurt.

No matter what Mig did over the years to erase the fact her mother had left and chosen not to be a part of her life, Leilani held tight-fisted to her abandonment issues.

Mig stood and pulled his daughter into a tight embrace. "I am not marrying Wimberly Ann. She's my friend, and I enjoy spending time with her. You have nothing to worry about, sweetheart."

He felt his shirt turn wet with her silent tears.

"There, there," he said as he patted her back. "Tell you what. Your papa will take you out to eat tonight, just the two of us. We'll catch up. You'll tell me all about that fancy job and let your makuakāne be impressed. After dinner, we'll go get some Dole Whip and sit by the ocean and watch the sun go down, just like old times."

She sniffed. "No Wimberly Ann?"

"Just the two of us," he repeated.

She pulled back and looked him in the eyes. "I don't have a good gut feeling on this one. I simply don't trust her, Papa."

Mig pushed a strand of wet hair from her face. "You don't have to trust Wimberly Ann, Leilana. You only have to trust me."

16

Christel grabbed a grocery cart and headed for the entrance to Costco. She fished her membership card, flashed it to the lady just inside the door, and then pushed her cart past a row of special deals. Despite being in a hurry, she stopped to check out a coupon special on Keurig cups. She used these at home and also at the office. This was a good buy.

When she was single, she rarely shopped at Costco. The quantities were often too much for one person. Heavens, the amounts were more than she and Evan could consume together, in many cases.

So why was she taking an hour out of her day to slug down the aisles? Evan loved the packages of thin-sliced salami. He adored the big tubs of hummus and the jars of specialty olives. His special soda was available in cases containing four flavors. Christel would traipse down these aisles any day to make him happy.

If things went their way, they would be pregnant by the end of the month. Perhaps she should start stocking up on formula and diapers. She might even pluck a few of those adorable soft onesies and toss them into her basket.

Now that the financial distraction at Pali Maui was primarily behind her, it seemed all she could think about was getting pregnant. She'd secretly purchased some maternity clothes and tucked them away—a cute pistachio green top with matching embroidered shorts that matched. Of course, there would be plenty of time to fill her closet before her belly forced her to exchange her current wardrobe, but she couldn't seem to quell her anticipation.

When Evan had sprung the news on her that he wanted to have a family right away, she'd felt panicked. She never made any huge decisions on a whim. Every option was carefully scrutinized with a mental list of pros and cons. Balance sheets served a purpose, not only for monetary transactions. Every move had a countermove, and Christel never liked to be surprised with unanticipated consequences.

Her brothers and sister teased that she was a control freak. Oh sure, she'd love to manipulate every aspect of life. That wasn't possible. More effective was the ability to plan the path ahead, so you didn't trip up on the journey.

Sadly, others had thrown a few roadblocks she'd been forced to step over. Even then, she'd laced up her proverbial sports shoes and tackled the obstacles head-on. Life was a mental game and she decided long ago to hold her chin up and charge ahead.

Christel wheeled her cart to the freezer aisles, where she plucked a lasagna and a bag of chicken wings and tossed them in her basket. She and Evan had busy schedules, and it was rare for them to cook on weeknights. They could, however, pluck something from the freezer and throw it in the oven.

She closed the freezer door and rounded the aisle. They also enjoyed nachos, and she needed shredded cheese.

"Oh!"

Christel looked up to find she'd nearly run into someone. "I'm so sorry. I wasn't looking."

She froze. The woman she'd come close to hitting with her cart was Mia Kané.

"Hello, Christel."

Christel blinked several times. Her ears thundered with immediate anger. "Excuse me." She redirected her cart and attempted to move around Mia. Unfortunately, an oncoming shopper blocked her success. Christel was forced to pause and wait.

"I hear the concert was a success," Mia said, her voice timid.

Christel glanced around. "Are you talking to me? I mean, you are going to stand there and pretend that nothing happened and simply have a conversation about the concert?"

Mia instantly teared up. "No—I was only…"

Christel glared. "You were only what?"

Mia's fingers trembled as she held the cart handle. "Nothing," she murmured. She pulled the cart back and turned in another direction.

Christel lost it.

She pushed her cart after Mia. "No, don't run. You wanted to what?"

It maddened her that Mia kept going and didn't turn around to answer. "I'm talking to you," she nearly screamed.

Mia flung around. "Stop. I know you hate me. I know Aiden hates me. I know Shane hates me…even though he's at least trying to be civil. I know your mother would rather eat shards of glass than be in the same room with me. I know!"

Christel pointed her finger like a weapon. "You only think you know. You have no idea. My dad is dead. Rotting in the ground. He was in a car accident coming home from your secret hideaway. He died smelling of your shampoo. Died with thoughts of your naked body against his. Died with the weight of adultery around his neck." She jabbed her finger again, not caring other customers were now watching. "He died because of you!"

"Do you think the guilt you are heaping on makes it any easier to lift my head? Do you have any idea what it feels like to wake each morning and the first thought you have is that you have let everyone you love down with your betrayal?" She angrily wiped at her wet eyes. "Do you know what it is like to face God's punishment for doing unspeakable wrong? I can say I'm sorry to everyone...to God...but I am the one who jabbed a needle in the eyes of my family and dearest friends. No amount of forgiveness will ever restore eyesight. The wounds will remain. Forever."

Mia was sobbing now.

A woman left her shopping cart and walked over. "Honey, is everything all right?"

Christel nearly shoved her. "We're fine. Can't you see we're fine?"

She directed her gaze to her former best friend and drew a deep, ragged breath. "You slept with my father, Mia."

The woman grew wide-eyed. "I—I'll just leave you two alone."

Christel gave her another warning look, and the lady scurried on down the aisle.

Mia's lip quivered. "Look, I don't want to cause any more pain."

Christel pulled her chest up and straightened her shoulders. "Fine. Let's just do our best to avoid one another until you go home."

Mia chewed at her lip several seconds before answering. "I am home."

"What?"

"I went back to the mainland, gave up my lease, and had my things shipped to the island. I'm going to take over the luau for Mom until she's up to it again. I know wanting her to be healed could be hopeful thinking, but regardless, I want to be here with her." She held up her hand to ward off any snide comment from Christel. "I may be a wretched human being on many levels, but I love my mother. I will do everything in my power to support her, to make up for all I've put her through."

Christel was speechless.

"I can't make you all forgive me. Frankly, it's not even necessary." Mia looked Christel straight in the eye. "But I am sorry for what I did. Terribly, terribly sorry."

Mia took hold of her cart and eased it forward, maneuvering around Christel.

Christel slowly turned and watched as Mia walked away.

Christel huffed.

She had every right to say those things—and certainly had not held back. She'd told her dad's mistress, her former best friend, exactly what she thought of her and how she felt about what she'd done to their family.

She'd gotten all of it off her chest. The hurt, the betrayal, the anger...left nothing unexpressed. Christel said everything she'd rehearsed in her head in the months after the affair was uncovered, all the things she wanted to say right to Mia's face. She'd said it all.

Christel looked down at her own hands and realized she was shaking.

Yes, she had certainly let Mia have it. That traitor deserved all of it.

Christel took a jagged, deep breath.

So, why did she feel so empty?

17

"Mia, baby. What's the matter? Your makuahine can tell something is bothering you."

Mia carried a pitcher of cold water to her mother's bedside. "Nothing, Mom. I'm fine."

She could tell by the worry in her mother's eyes that her statement had fallen flat. Her mom knew her better than almost anyone. Nothing could be hidden from her mother's scrutiny.

From the time she was little, her mom had the uncanny ability to know things. Once, when she was about seven years old, she came home from school nearly in tears—not because she had done poorly on a test, but because her revered teacher had failed to praise her for the accomplishment.

With one look, her mother nodded slowly and said, "Mrs. Cameron must've been so proud of you." She waited, watched.

When Mia crumpled and began crying, her mom took her in her arms. "Mia, you must never seek your worth in others. People are broken and will always let you down. Even your parents, who love you dearly, will fail you. Only look to your Creator, who knitted you in my womb and gave you purpose."

Her mother cupped her little-girl chin. "When you hurt...reach for him and he will lift you up."

Mia now felt the same message coming from her mother's eyes. While she had not heard the venom in Christel's voice, she was filled with understanding.

She knew...maybe not the details, but she knew.

CHRISTEL SLAMMED the bags onto the kitchen counter and opened a cupboard door with enough force to nearly pull it from its hinges. She plucked several cans from the bags, shoved them onto the shelves, then slammed the door shut.

After grabbing the salami, she marched to the refrigerator, pulled the door open, and tossed the package inside the deli drawer. She slammed the drawer shut with her hip, then the refrigerator door.

"Hey, what's going on?" A freshly shaved Evan appeared, wiping his hands on a towel. "You okay?"

"Do I look like I'm okay?" she said, not bothering to temper her snark.

Evan watched her, puzzled. "Did something happen?"

Christel swung around to face him. "You might say that."

Evan tossed the towel to the counter. "Want to talk about it?"

Christel fisted her hands at her sides. "Not particularly. Let's just say I had a little run-in with the person I most detest."

Evan stood, wisely remaining silent. His look urged her on.

"I hate her!" Christel screamed. "I hate her."

Her shoulders were now trembling, and she sensed that at any moment, she might break. Taking a deep breath, she struggled for control.

Christel dug in the back and pulled a bag of chips. Evan's eyes followed her movements as if he worried about what might happen to the chips if she genuinely lost it. They both knew she was on the edge. Anything could happen.

Evan reached and took her by the hand. She carried the bag of chips and followed him to the sofa.

"Sit." He pulled her down beside him. "Spill. From the beginning."

She told him about the unexpected meet-up with Mia in Costco and recited word-for-word their exchange. One of the character traits that made her an excellent attorney and accountant was her trap mind for detail. She remembered every word and left nothing out.

When she'd finished, she looked her husband in the eye. "If she wondered how I felt before, she no longer has to ponder the matter."

She caught him in a smirk. "Stop, it's not funny."

He held up open palms. "No, but I was just considering what security was thinking as they viewed the film. They didn't show up to intervene, so I assume they were uneasy and didn't think it wise to intervene." He laughed out loud. "I'm just saying."

Christel couldn't help it. The mental image of a couple of uniformed fat guys in some office eating popcorn while watching her yell at the top of her lungs was comical. The footage would likely be endless entertainment as bored security officials viewed the soap opera-like exchange repeatedly.

"How do you do that?" she asked her husband, smiling.

He laced his fingers with hers. "Do what?"

"How do you surgically excise my emotions and cut out the extraneous, hurtful parts and leave me whole again?" She smiled at him. "It's as if you had training."

"I don't know about that." He took the bag of chips from her other hand and tossed it to the floor before leaning in close. He touched her lips softly with his, gently.

Her eyes closed as she savored the wonderful scent of his cologne. She felt safe with him.

Evan's arms tightened around her as he pressed more firmly against her lips. Hers opened, and his breath caught as he opened his mouth to her, holding her against him as though he would never let go.

Feeling the strength in those muscular arms around her, Christel let herself sink into a good, heartfelt cry. Tears came tentatively, at first...then with more force. She was fully aware of him, but what mattered to her at the moment was that for the first time since losing her father to the tragic accident, she could completely let go.

And she wasn't alone.

Evan rocked her gently as tears purged the ache, the loneliness, the wounds of betrayal by two of the people she most loved in the world...her father and her best friend.

She wasn't sure how many minutes passed before her weeping slowed to a sniffle, then a murmur against his chest. She lifted her head and looked at him, though she said nothing. Her brain was numb.

He kissed her again, holding her against him. She felt his own need...heard his tortured moan.

Over the next moments, they both gave themselves to one another, surrendering their needs and knowing they would be filled.

Somewhere over the span of those moments, Christel let go. She was full. Mia would not hurt her anymore.

18

Ava gingerly made her way across the rock pathway to Alani's back garden. Her best friend spotted her from where she sat in an Adirondack chair wearing a chenille robe with a light blanket draped over her lap.

"Hey," she said, smiling. "I hoped you'd come today."

Ava scowled. "Why wouldn't I come? I'm here every Monday, Wednesday, and Friday and often a few weekend mornings." She leaned over and brushed a kiss against Alani's sunken cheek. "Love the wig," she said, winking.

"You do? Well, you should. When we unboxed this long thing, I immediately thought you'd gone nuts." A tiny grin sprouted. "But I've grown to like the 'old girl…red and all."

"The hair color matches your feisty spirit, my friend."

"Ha, I don't know about that. My feisty is a bit fizzled these days." Alani motioned for her to sit in the chair next to her. "What's that?" She pointed to the bag Ava carried.

Ava grinned and held up the plastic grocery sack. "What? This?"

Alani rolled her eyes. "Yes. That."

Ava dropped the bag to her lap and opened it. She

retrieved several books and held them up on display. "These are novels. I know you say you never have time to read, but I thought maybe you might capture some of this downtime and dig into a few stories. I have an excellent mystery, a legal thriller, and a couple of romances. Nothing too risqué, of course. Oh, and I brought you some novels by Sheila Roberts. I just love her feel-good stories. You can count on a happy ending in her books."

Alani reached for the happy books. "Those look to be right up my alley these days. Nothing sad."

Ava placed the stack on the outdoor table as Mia opened the back door and brought them a tray filled with a pitcher of iced tea with some glasses. "This is mango iced tea, purchased directly from that little store in Lahaina. You know the one, Mom. We shopped there a lot."

Alani nodded. "I know just the one you're speaking of. Shara Okeima owns the place. She also sells those little Nani purses I love so much."

Mia turned to Ava. "I hope you like the tea."

Ava forced a smile. "Thank you. I'm sure I will." While the relationship with her best friend's daughter would never return to what it had been before discovering her betrayal, Ava decided to move on from the anger…for Alani's sake. Thankfully, every encounter became more easy and less painful.

She noticed Mia's hand tremble as she filled her mother's glass.

Likely, it was difficult for Mia to face her as well. One thing remained true…sin was the gift that kept on giving.

When Mia left, Alani quickly covered Ava's hand with her own. "Thank you," she mouthed.

Ava simply nodded and gave her friend a slight smile.

Over the next hour, they drank their tea and chatted. It was almost like the times before Alani's cancer. The two of them would start talking, and before she knew it, hours had passed.

"Let a girl live vicarious through you. Update and tell me all about Tom," Alani urged.

Ava immediately blushed. Even mentioning his name sent her blood racing, her heart pounding, and her palms sweaty. She felt like a schoolgirl with a crush on the high school jock all the girls longed to date.

Only she didn't have to share Tom. He only had eyes for her.

"Aye, see that look in your eyes? You are completely twitterpated." The term referred to one of their favorite scenes in Disney's Bambi movie.

"I am not," Ava argued, but not very convincing.

"Details. I want details." Alani leaned close. "Don't leave anything out."

Where should Ava start? There was no denying she was falling hard for the architect she'd hired to renovate the golf course at Pali Maui. How could she begin to convey the number of times she thought of him daily? Or the mornings she awoke, dreaming of the two of them wrapped in each other's arms?

Sadly, she still had occasional nightmares, too. Times where she woke in a cold sweat after looking down at Lincoln in the casket with the piece of paper stuck in his suit pocket. Once, her subconscious mind conjured him sitting up and telling her he loved Mia.

Ava gave her friend a wide grin, hiding the uninvited thoughts that crept into her mind. "What can I say? Tom Strobe is simply wonderful, Alani."

She noted the look of anticipation on her friend's face and laughed. "Sounds like you need to be reading a few of those romance novels...get your fix."

Alani shrugged and let out a giggle. "What can I say? Even without hair and little to no appetite, I'm a hopeless romantic."

"We went fishing the other day," Ava told her.

"Fishing? I thought you hated to fish."

"Hate is a strong word, don't you think? Besides, it's easy to enjoy fishing when you get to stand next to a guy who smells like Tom Strobe." She winked. "Normally, I fish from Jack's boat, but Tom took me to Kahului Harbor and we cast from the shoreline. We caught all sorts of species, including triggerfish, goatfish, and trevally. Afterward, we went to his place and he cooked up our catch. I fell in love with the trevally. In all the years I've lived in Maui, I'm not sure I'd ever eaten it before."

Alani waved off her comment. "Of course, you have. We serve it at Te Au Kané Luau frequently. I'm sure you've had some."

"Maybe," Ava agreed. "But no one at the luau has ever fed bites to me on a fork." She grinned. "Just like in the movies."

Alani clasped her hands. "Now, that is romantic."

Her friend refilled her glass from the pitcher. "Is he a good kisser? Elta is such a good kisser." She closed her eyes and smiled. "I still remember the first time. We were in the church parking lot."

"The church parking lot?" Ava placed her hand across her chest in shock. "Such scandal!"

"Oh, that kiss was a little bit of heaven right here on earth. I still feel rocketed into the atmosphere when he kisses me goodnight."

Ava grew wistful. She missed having someone next to her in bed at night.

Alani seemed to pick up on her feelings and patted her leg. "God is not done in that department, my friend. You just wait and see. Maybe it'll be Tom Strobe, or perhaps someone you haven't even met yet, but God is the author of romance, and he's still writing your story."

Ava let out a heavy sigh.

Alani wiggled her fingers at her. "Stop that stinking thinking. Just because Lincoln hurt you doesn't mean a future mate will do the same. Open your heart to the possibilities, my dear friend."

She paused and warned, "Ava, I mean it. Don't hold back when it comes to matters of the heart." She picked at the blanket on her lap.

"None of us is promised tomorrow."

19

Leilani Nakamoa shut down the engine of her rental car and sat staring at the open house sign. While her stomach was filled with butterflies, she was convinced she was doing the right thing.

After several sleepless nights, she'd finally decided she had no choice but to confront the situation head-on.

She reached for her Louis Vuitton bag and climbed from the car.

The house was a multi-unit condominium in Kihei, newly renovated with a distant ocean view. Based on the price tag, the selling realtor stood to make a tidy profit.

Wimberly Ann wouldn't have to sell many properties to fill her bank account. Of course, living expenses on the island could drain any reserves. In addition to regular expenditures, Wimberly Ann's allotment for hair dye, eyebrow waxes, and those dagger fingernails had to be big-budget items.

At least Wimberly Ann's clothing budget wouldn't be a problem. Frankly, the woman her dad was dating looked like she'd just walked off a 1970s television game show. Someone needed to tell her shoulder pads were no longer in style. Don't even start with how she rode into the room on a cloud of saccharine perfume.

Those chest humps? Well, those couldn't possibly be real.

In her line of work, Leilani was very familiar with women on the hunt. Wimberly Ann had likely sold her soul so many times that no one would buy it anymore. No one except Leilani's lonely father, who could be horribly gullible.

Her father always viewed people from one side. Rarely did he examine a person's true nature and see the manipulation and selfishness she saw in public relations. It was rare to encounter an individual who wasn't trying to con the system in some manner, trying to conjure a way to make a profit on the vulnerabilities of others.

That didn't make someone evil, necessarily. Heavens, she made her living utilizing every tool to build brands and convey images that were rarely authentic.

What she did have a problem with was when a woman tried to rope a lonely man who had substantial resources, financial and otherwise, into marrying them.

Leilani pulled her shoulders straight. No woman who was married six times prior was going to take advantage of her father—a woman who was a serial gold digger. Not on her watch.

She marched up the path to the front door. Thankfully, no other cars were parked out front—no prospective buyers to maneuver as she met with this woman face-to-face for a little talk.

Leilani reached for the doorknob as the door swung open.

"Welcome," Wimberly Ann blurted in a sing-song voice that rivaled that of an appliance sales associate down at the former Sears store. The realtor's brows knit together. Clearly, she recognized Leilani but couldn't place her.

Suddenly, realization dawned that Mig's daughter stood before her.

"Leilani? What are you doing here?" She swept her arm in a motion that invited her inside.

A glance around revealed an open and airy floorplan with lots of windows.

"Are you shopping for real estate? Your dad will be delighted to know you..."

"Cut the crap," Leilani barked. "I'm not here to buy a condo. I'm here to tell you I'm on to you."

Wimberly Ann's bright red lips dropped open, speechless.

"Perhaps he's too naïve to trace your history and see the long trail of husbands you've left behind, but make no mistake...I'm not someone you can slip by. I know who you are." She jabbed a finger in Wimberly Ann's direction.

"I...I'm sorry. I don't know what to say," Wimberly Ann muttered.

"You don't need to say anything. Just know this....Mig Nakamoa will not be your next sugar daddy. Got that?"

Leilani braced herself for the retort she knew was coming. She crossed her arms across her chest and waited.

"Would you like to come in and sit down?" Wimberly Ann stepped back and motioned for the sofa.

"In case you haven't clued in, this is not a friendly visit. This is your warning to stay as far away from my father as you can get." Leilani narrowed her eyes. "Or else."

She didn't know what her 'or else' was...or what she might do if this broad didn't scare easily and continued to chase after her dad. She hadn't stopped to consider the consequences if she failed to separate this gold-digger from her plans to hook up with her father. Her one chance, it seemed, was to project enough menace that her message was received as intended.

Wimberly Ann strolled casually to the sofa and sat. She patted the place next to her.

Leilani refused the offer and continued to stand with her arms crossed.

"I think there's been a huge misunderstanding," Wimberly Ann began. "First of all, let me assure you that while your tone is a bit off-putting, I think I understand your motive."

Leilani stared at the woman's bright red toes peeking from her sandals. "Oh, you do, do you?" She huffed. "Good. Then you catch my drift. I want you to stay away from my dad," she repeated, pausing between each word for emphasis.

Wimberly Ann smiled. "I applaud your attempt to protect Mig. He's a wonderful man, and he deserves your arduous protection."

Leilani was a little taken aback. This was not the response she'd expected. Of course, Wimberly Ann had not enticed six men into matrimony without being very cunning.

"Your patronizing will not win me over," she announced. "I have a closet full of Scrabble and Connect Four.....if you want to play games. But I suggest you get real."

"Please, sit." Wimberly Ann patted the seat beside her. "Clearly, you have a lot on your mind. Many questions. I'm happy to answer them all."

The comment pulled the wind out of Leilani's sails. She reluctantly dropped into a chair across from her anointed enemy.

"Good. Let's start with this—would you be as enamored with my father if there was an iron-clad prenuptial in place? What if you had no access to any of his bank accounts? By the way, I am on all his accounts. Believe me; I monitor them carefully."

"Then you know that Mig has spent very little on this relationship in terms of money." Wimberly Ann tucked a blonde tendril behind her ear. "I am not after your father's money. In fact, I don't even know if he has money...and it doesn't matter. I have my own—plenty, in fact."

She stood and retrieved a Mac from her briefcase, logged

on, and turned the screen to Leilani. "I'm an open book. This is only one of my accounts."

Leilani's eyes widened. Her curiosity would not let her turn away. She stared at the computer screen. What she saw took her breath away.

"You have millions in that account," she whispered incredulously. "Where did you get all that money? You're a realtor."

Wimberly Ann quickly defended herself. "Realtors do quite well if they are good at their profession, and I am. But that is not where the money came from."

Wimberly Ann's breath caught in her throat. This meeting was taking a turn she wasn't prepared for.

"I'm from Arkansas," Wimberly Ann explained. "I spent more than one holiday around the Walton family Christmas tree." She paused to let the information sink in. "I live by a little motto: Money talks, but real wealth whispers. Second, my personal business is just that...my personal business."

Leilani couldn't help it. Her eyes went wide. She swallowed. "Does Dad know?"

"Yes. I don't keep anything from your father."

Leilani fought to breathe. "I...I don't know what to say."

Wimberly Ann's face softened. "You can say you won't bring this matter up again...and that this little meeting will remain just between the two of us."

Leilani's eyes filled with tears. She'd been awful...plain awful. How could she have jumped to those conclusions? How could she think she had the right to march in here and confront Wimberly Ann?

She was embarrassed and ashamed. "Why...I mean, you could date anyone. Why my dad?"

The woman leaned forward, ever so slightly. "Your father is the most genuine, charming, lovely man I've ever met. He's hardworking. He treats everyone, especially those who report to him, with extreme kindness. He's extremely smart, incredibly funny, and enjoyable to be around. He treats me like a queen." She smiled. "I could go on."

Leilani slowly brought her hand to her mouth. "I—I feel like a fool."

Wimberly Ann stood and moved to her side. She placed her manicured nail on Leilani's shoulder. "I know you wanted to protect your father."

"But I was awful to you."

Wimberly Ann gently nodded. "Yes, maybe you were. Like I said, your intentions were to shield your father. I know that. Let's just agree to leave this right here."

Leilani sniffed. "I thought you said you didn't keep secrets from him."

"Like you, I think Mig is worthy of protection. I wouldn't ever want to be the impetus of any conflict between the two of you." Her face broke into a warm, forgiving smile. "Let's seal the deal and agree to move forward and be friends." She patted Leilani's shoulder.

Leilani stood. "You deserve my apology. I misunderstood… well, everything."

Wimberly Ann tossed her blonde head back and laughed. "Well, you know what they say—it costs a lot of money to look this cheap. Believe me, I'm not as silly as I look. I know what I want. I don't count my money. I count my blessings." Her expression turned soft. "Your father is just that…a blessing."

Wimberly Ann took Leilani's hand and squeezed. "I've weathered some real pickles when it comes to men. Your father is different. I am grateful he's decided to spend time with me. What the future holds? Who knows? What I do know is that I'll always have his best interests at heart."

Wimberly Ann looked Leilani straight in the eye.

"You have my promise."

True to her word, Wimberly Ann never mentioned Leilani's little visit. In the days that followed, Leilani significantly altered her earlier attitude and offered to take her dad and his new friend to dinner at No Ka 'Oi, where they enjoyed Jon's culinary skills.

Her dad rarely deviated from his favorite pan-seared gingered salmon. On the suggestion of Wimberly Ann, he ventured out of his norm and ordered Lau Lau, an island favorite made of fish and pork marinated and steamed in taro leaves. For dessert, they shared a dark chocolate tart. Leilani didn't even cringe when Wimberly Ann placed a fresh raspberry inside her father's mouth. In fact, she almost enjoyed seeing the look that passed between them.

Wimberly Ann also accompanied them to the airport when it was time for Leilani to fly home. No matter the fact that she had a rental car, her father always insisted on being at the terminal to send her off.

Wimberly Ann drew Leilani into a hug. "It was so nice to meet you finally."

"Same," Leilani told her, returning the embrace. "I hope we get to see one another soon."

Leilani turned and kissed her dad on the cheek, whispering, "I'm glad you're happy, Dad."

She stepped back and grabbed her suitcase.

"Don't stay away so long this time." Mig raised his head, looked at her, and expectantly arched his brows, awaiting her reply.

Leilani's heart filled. "I won't. I love you, Dad."

"I love you, too."

She turned to get in line at security when she suddenly stopped and looked back at Wimberly Ann. Her father's friend was dressed in hot pink ankle pants with a matching polka dot top with frilly ruffles at the neckline and a stack of cheap-looking bangle bracelets on her wrist.

Leilani's face drew into a smile. "Take care of him."

Wimberly Ann winked. "You know I will."

20

As summer turned into early fall, tourists continued to flock to the island. Thanks to an extensive social media campaign and word of mouth, many of them found their way to Pali Maui. They filled the tour buses, where knowledgeable guides explained the planting and harvesting techniques and showed how the plantation workers still cultivated the fruit by hand, and enjoyed samples of the hand-picked, machete-cut pineapple straight from the fields.

After exploring the plantation, guests found their way to an exclusive lunch at No Ka 'Oi and then loaded their shopping carts at the gift shop.

Thanks to all this and the monthly outdoor concerts, Pali Maui's cash flow problems were resolved, and the revenue needed to meet payroll and pay for operating expenses was satisfied.

The damage from the storm had all been remedied. For the most part, activities returned to normal.

Ava edged to the gift shop, coffee in hand.

"Morning, sweetheart," she said, entering through the door propped open with a stone painted with the word ALOHA.

Katie smiled from behind the counter. "Hi, Mom." She grinned and pointed to a stack of unopened boxes next to the back wall. "You're just in time to help me inventory our incoming merchandise. I can't wait for you to see the line of jewelry I'm adding. Every piece is hand-crafted." Katie lifted her hand for her mother's inspection. "Look at this hono sea turtle crafted out of Mother-of-pearl and jade."

Ava leaned close for a better look. "I love it." She lifted her gaze to her daughter. "Katie, I am so proud of you and what you've done. You have a tremendous acumen for marketing. Pali Maui wouldn't have made it through this past difficulty without you."

Her daughter radiated with pride. "Thanks, Mom."

A car engine caught both of their attention. Ava looked out the open door, and her face immediately broke into a pleased smile as she saw Tom climb from his vehicle.

He waved and joined them inside.

"Hi, Tom," Katie said as she got out the box cutter.

He held up open palms and laughed. "Is it something I said?"

Puzzled, Katie studied the sharp blade for a moment.

"Honey, it's a joke," Ava told her with a pat on the back.

"Oh." Katie frowned. "Funny...I guess." She looked at her mother. "I suppose this means I get to put the inventory away on my own?" She gave the couple a quick wink and a grin.

"Yes, that is exactly what it means." Ava linked arms with Tom. "We have to go and look at the new clubhouse patio. They poured the cement last night, and I'm dying for a peek at how things turned out."

It went unsaid that she could've wandered over herself to inspect the progress. Why not wait and take the opportunity to see it with Tom? Ava smiled to herself. Everything was better when shared with Tom.

Despite the setbacks caused by the storm and the damage

to the golf course, the renovation was finally nearing completion. Tom had estimated they could safely schedule the grand reopening at the beginning of next month, less than four weeks away.

"I am so happy with how this all turned out," she told Tom as they walked toward the first tee-box. "Truly, the results far surpassed my highest expectations."

Tom slipped his fingers through hers and squeezed. "I think Pali Maui may be my best work," he told her, which was saying a lot given his reputation. Ava wasn't sure how many projects he'd completed, but Tom had designed some of the most famous golf courses in the PGA. Golf Digest had contacted her and arranged a photo shoot and planned to feature an article showcasing his recent achievement.

Suddenly, Tom stopped walking. He turned to her. "Look, now that things are back on track and we're in the final cleanup stage, I've got something I've been wanting to ask you."

Her eyebrows lifted. "What is it?"

"I have to make a trip to Boston. It's my mother's eightieth birthday. I'd like you to go with me." He draped an arm around her shoulders and pulled her against him. "What do you say? Are you up for a long weekend away?"

She opened her mouth to protest. How could she possibly leave Pali Maui when the new harvest was about to begin? The list was long when it came to all the tasks she needed to complete in time for the grand re-opening event for the golf course. Katie would have a cow if she dropped the entire event in her lap.

There was no way she could walk away from all this responsibility. Yet, when she opened her mouth to report that fact to Tom, something in the look on his face made her hesitate.

"Don't say no," he pleaded. "It's only a couple of days. Besides, I can't stand the idea of being that far away from you, even for a short time. Please say yes."

She, too, could not fathom being a continent away from the person who made her heart race a little every time she saw him. Three or four days could feel like a lifetime without seeing his blue SUV winding its way up the drive.

Ava sucked in a breath. She was torn.

Tom gave her shoulders another tight squeeze. "Just say yes. It'll be fun. Well, maybe not the family obligation part, but a trip away might be just the ticket. You work so hard, Ava. A mini-vacation will do you good."

She opened her mouth and was surprised to hear herself say, "Okay, sure." Not only did those words fail to reconcile with her anxiety over leaving things unattended here at Pali Maui, but an overnight trip presented another cause for consternation.

She and Tom had been romantically involved for months, yet a clear boundary remained. They had never slept together. It was left unspoken that she wasn't ready for such a leap. Thankfully, Tom was far too much a gentleman to push the issue.

Call her old-fashioned, and she was, but Ava believed sexual intimacy was best enjoyed within the confines of marriage. Besides, it was still too soon after Lincoln's death. Her husband was the only man she'd ever been with in that way. She simply wasn't ready to venture into a new intimate relationship, even if the thought of being with Tom was secretly exciting.

Never mind how it would look to her daughters, and her granddaughters...and Alani. Her best friend would have a fit! No pastor's wife worth her salt would give a pat of acceptance on what she thought to be sin.

When the subject last came up after a movie they'd seen, Alani drew her hefty shoulders up like a soldier and huffed. "I simply do not know what has gotten into society. It seems like everywhere you turn, the slither has met the slime."

Alani's straight-laced attitude only served to heighten the pain resulting from what her daughter and Lincoln had done.

It was then that Ava realized Tom was talking and she hadn't been listening. "I'm sorry. What did you say?"

"I said I'd get the tickets and alert Mother we're coming."

And just like that, Ava was going on a trip.

With Tom.

To meet his mother.

21

Christel gazed at the plastic wand in her hand and the lack of line which confirmed her worst fear...she was still not pregnant.

Her ears rang with anger. She looked at herself in the bathroom mirror and immediately burst into tears.

Evan banged on the closed door. "Christel, honey? Are you okay?"

Hard as she tried, she failed to muster enough focus to respond. All she could do was whimper a pitiful, "Yes."

He jiggled the locked door. "Honey, open the door."

For a brief moment, she considered not complying with his request. All she wanted to do was to slump to the floor and have herself a good cry...a well-deserved breakdown.

She tossed the wand into the garbage with more force than she intended, creating a loud clang as plastic hit metal.

For months, she'd been crossing days off her calendar and waiting with bated breath for yet another opportunity to pee onto the tiny tool that would reveal the news that would rocket her to the moon with elation, or dash her into the pit of despair.

Evan rattled the door again. "Christel, I mean it. Open up."

The tone in his voice made it clear she couldn't hold him off much longer. Not without inviting conflict. There was enough of that already.

Christel married Evan knowing he was nothing like Jay. He didn't lie. He told the truth. He didn't spend all their money and try to hide it. He willingly shared his financial resources with her by placing her name on all his accounts, and they were many. He didn't stay out all night, leaving her to sweat with worry. Instead, he came directly home from the hospital and willingly spent every free moment with her. Small talk was as important to him as eating and he happily delved into any topic she wished. They even had long discussions pertaining to equities, derivatives, futures, commodities, and forex markets. Never mind she constantly changed the subject when the topic turned to anything medically related. Surgical terms and complicated anatomical anomalies made her feel cerebrally clumsy, like Bambi learning to walk.

Unlike Jay, who created his own storm and then complained when it rained, Evan was her shelter, her soul mate. His arms had become home to her.

So, why then, did she feel trapped when he said he wanted a family?

It's not that she did not want to be a mother. She did.

After Jay, she'd convinced herself that children were on the distant shore. Now, she felt compelled to climb onto the fertility boat and row like crazy. No matter how hard and fast she paddled, waves of defeat pushed her back and she was no closer to sliding booties on an infant's foot than she was months ago.

She felt like a failure.

Worse, she was letting Evan down.

Christel slid the back of her hand across her teary eyes. "Just a minute," she called out.

She drew a deep breath, convinced she could steady herself and hide the emotions that threatened to pull her under.

With a trembling hand, she reached and opened the door.

On the other side, Evan stood with worry etched across his face. "Christel?"

One look and he knew. She'd been foolish to think she could hide her crumbling emotions.

"Oh, baby." He drew her into her arms and held her tight, holding her like that for several minutes before he finally pulled back and lifted her chin.

"Honey, it's time."

Christel swallowed, knowing full well what he meant. She said nothing. She didn't need to.

"I'll call and make the appointment with Dr. Varghese. There is no better fertility specialist in Hawaii. If she recommends it, we'll take you to the mainland and find additional medical help. No test will be spared. No procedure. No effort."

He slowly wiped the moisture from her mottled cheek. "We'll get you pregnant by Christmas. I promise."

Christel nodded, knowing his confidence was a pipe dream. Sure, Evan was a highly trained surgeon with years of education and practice to back up any assertion. Despite all that, she knew even he couldn't guarantee absolute success. No one could.

She could barely hold up under the pressure.

What if something was wrong with her? What if she'd waited too long and she was now too old to conceive? What if she couldn't get pregnant and give her husband the children he longed for?

She squeezed her eyes shut against an even worse possibility.

If she couldn't give him a family, would Evan be sorry he'd married her?

22

Ava picked up the remote and clicked off the news. It had been a long day filled with online meetings with shippers and buyers alerting business associates that Pali Maui was back in business. As satisfying as the announcements were, she knew the work that would bring.

She had no business considering taking a trip to Boston right now. Her mental list of pros and cons tipped heavily to the side of passing on Tom's invitation. Yet, a tiny voice inside told her she needed to throw caution and reasoning to the wind and go.

Even Alani told her she'd be a fool to decline to take this trip. "This is the next step in a relationship, Ava. Meeting his family. Don't hold back and hope opportunity will jump in your path again...especially when it comes to relationships." She wagged her plump finger. "Aloha Mai No. It means: I give my love to you, you give your love to me. Love is a two-way street, my friend. This is your turn to step out of your comfort zone and show Tom he is important to you."

Ava hugged her dear friend as they walked along the beach. "Are you getting tired?"

Alani waved her off. "Don't change the subject. And no, I'm not getting tired. The doctors are encouraging me to exercise and get my strength back." She grinned and winked. "That 'ole cancer thought it had me. I think the good Lord had another plan."

Ava stood and grabbed her iced tea glass, and headed for the sink. She'd always admired Alani, even more now after watching her battle cancer with such grace and dignity. Even when things got hard, her faith never wavered from her mantra: Healed or Heaven. No matter how things turned out, she was at peace.

If only she could emulate Alani's attitude and do the same.

A loud banging on her door pulled her attention. She frowned. Who could that possibly be at this time of night?

Ava tossed her remaining tea in the sink, set her glass on the counter, and then moved for the door. "Okay, okay...I'm coming," she hollered as the pounding continued.

She opened the door to find Vanessa. Her sister did not wait to be invited in before pushing past Ava and into the house.

"Vanessa?"

"You won't believe what happened!" Her sister tossed her Louis Vuitton on the sofa and plopped down beside it. "Truly, you won't believe it."

Vanessa's smudged eye makeup suggested she'd been crying. Her face was mottled despite the heavy layer of perfectly applied foundation.

Ava frowned. "Well, if I'm going to believe it, you will have to spill and tell me what it is." She took a deep breath, knowing she sounded a little sharp. Not that she didn't care about her sister's woes, but Vanessa was known for being a drama queen. Things others would let roll off their backs were monumental spectacles in Vanessa's world.

"He fired me!"

"Who fired you?"

"Jim Kahale." Fresh tears sprouted, followed by ragged breathing. "Can you believe that? After everything I've done for him and that campaign. He wouldn't even be off the ground in terms of public exposure had it not been for me." Her jaw set, and anger now flashed in her eyes.

Ava's hand went to her chest. "What happened?"

"What happened is that his disco stick went dancing with someone else."

"Vanessa!"

Vanessa huffed. "What? Lady Gaga…"

"Don't be crass," Ava warned. "It's unbecoming."

Vanessa rolled her eyes. Clearly, she believed Ava was far too straightlaced.

Her sister crossed her arms against her chest. "Jim had the nerve to announce that he was making this new chick his campaign manager. I'd be reporting to her!"

Ava wandered back into the living room, with Vanessa following closely behind. She motioned for her sister to sit. "Is that a bad thing?"

"Of course, it's a bad thing." She lifted her forefinger. "One, I'm not going to be in a position where I have to go through filters to get to Jim." She raised a second finger. "Two, I'm not going to have someone else weighing in on my recommendations". And another. "Three, I'm not going to have to get approval for marketing expenditures." She raised a final finger. "And I'm certainly not going to have to report to some woman who knows less than half of the knowledge I have in my pinky finger," She nearly growled. "Do you know what she did before this?"

Ava silently shook her head.

"Jim's new hire ran a surf shop. It wasn't even her surf shop. She ran it for someone else." Vanessa pounded her knee. "The girl is blonde, has long tan legs, and has blue eyes the color of Honolua Bay. She got this job by sleeping with Jim."

Ava refrained from reminding Vanessa that she had done the same.

"So, I gave him an ultimatum. Either her or me."

"And he chose her," Ava said quietly.

"He'll be sorry," Vanessa nearly screamed. "Believe me… he'll regret that decision."

Ava swallowed. "Well, Vanessa. I am truly sorry that happened to you."

Vanessa pursed her lips. "There is something you can do."

Ava braced. Here it comes, she thought.

"I need to move back in with you," Vanessa told her. "Temporarily. I can't make rent without a job. I know the shanty you lent me is now occupied, but I could stay in your guest room. Again, just for a while…until I figure something out."

Ava's hands drew into fists at her side. No matter what path Vanessa took in life, it always ended up here…with Ava having to pick up the pieces and the mess she'd made. True, her sister couldn't exactly be held responsible for Jim's decision, but Ava had warned her. No good would ever come from working for someone you had been intimate with…romantically, and physically.

As always, Vanessa had brushed off her advice and moved forward without regard for using good sense.

"Okay, I can see from your eyes that you are judging me. You always judge me!" Vanessa complained. "Can't you ever just be my sister and offer support without that look?"

Ava blinked a couple of times, mentally hoping to close the window into her thoughts. "I'm not judging you," she argued.

"Yes, you are."

Ava took a deep breath, wrestling a twinge of guilt. "Look, you can stay for a few weeks, but only a few weeks. I'm going to Boston, and you can house sit. But after that, you need to find a place of your own. This is not permanent. This offer is not even meant to extend to a month. Is that clear?"

"You're going to Boston?"

"With Tom," Ava clarified.

And just like that, her decision was made. She'd go with him to celebrate his mother's birthday.

23

Ava sat anxiously with her packed luggage by her front door waiting for Jack to show up.

She should have known better than to count on her older brother to be on time. Captain Jack, as he was commonly known on the island, had little regard for punctuality. When taking tourists out for boating excursions, his reputation was to launch the Canefire from the dock much later than the brochures advertised.

When she learned Tom had an early morning meeting in Kahului, Ava made a snap judgment and told him he didn't need to pick her up. She'd simply meet him at the airport. After hanging up from the telephone call, she remembered her vehicle was in for service.

Her kids and Mig had obligations that would not make it convenient to taxi her to the airport. She had little choice but to turn to Jack.

Ava grabbed her phone from her bag and scrolled through her contacts, looking for his number, when she saw his beat-up 1978 Chevy Silverado coming up the lane. As he neared, the vintage pickup sputtered and backfired twice before he finally pulled to a stop in front of her house.

With a relieved breath, she slipped her purse straps onto her shoulder and hurried for the door, opening it before Jack could toss his cigar butt into her manicured yard. "Thought you'd never get here," she said, nearly breathless. "What took you so long?"

Jack's eyes twinkled as he cleared his throat. "Had an overnight lady guest, and our morning goodbyes took a little longer than intended." He winked and let out a laugh.

Ava punched her brother on the arm. "Well, glad to know your love life is flourishing. Mine, however, is on a tightrope. Mind if we get this show on the road, so I don't miss my flight and ruin my relationship?"

He let out another loud laugh as he picked up her suitcase and led her to his pickup. Minutes later, they were on their way.

"So, you're going to meet his family," Jack said with a chuckle. "Sounds serious." Without waiting for her response, he leaned over and turned on the radio. A Beethoven melody filled the truck.

Her crusty brother was nothing if not a bundle of contradictions. His adventurous lifestyle filled with all-nighters down at the Dirty Monkey represented one side of the coin. His love of tiny kittens and classical music, the other.

"It's nothing, really. His mother is turning eighty, and Tom didn't want to go to Boston alone."

The corners of her brother's lips lifted in a wide grin. "Uh, huh."

"Jack, we're taking this slow."

"You sleeping with him?"

The question caused her breath to catch. "Seriously? You think my sex life is your business?"

He laughed while lifting his shoulders in an exaggerated shrug. Her brother held a very loose notion of propriety. To him, life was a ripe peach waiting to be consumed in a manner that left juice running down the corners of his lips.

"Lighten up, sis," he told her. "You're far too young to put the mare in the barn."

Hoping to change the subject, she pulled out her phone and checked her digital airline ticket. "We're running a little late."

Jack heard that and punched the gas pedal. The truck lurched forward and sped down the highway. "Don't worry. 'Ole Jack never lets a woman down."

At the airport, Tom was standing on the sidewalk waiting. As soon as he spotted her climbing from Jack's pickup, he waved.

"You made it," he said, helping her with her luggage.

"Yup. Got her here safe and sound," Jack said, chewing on his unlit cigar. He squeezed his sister's shoulders. "Now, be careful and don't stay out late. In those big cities, the only things open after midnight are legs and hospitals."

THE FLIGHT from Maui to Boston was long, over ten hours. When they landed, a town car was waiting, the first sign that Tom's family had money.

The second was learning his mother's home was located in Beacon Hill, one of the oldest neighborhoods in Boston, filled with brick sidewalks, antique gas lamps, and multi-million dollar Federal-style row houses with ivy growing up the brick.

Tom's mother, Frances Strobe, lived in one of the most prestigious residences in the area, situated within walking distance of the Charles River. Her neighbors included John Kerry, Teresa Heinz, Carly Simon, and the descendants of well-known author, Louisa May Alcott.

"You grew up here?" Ava asked, her eyes wide with surprise.

She knew Tom didn't want for money, but would never have guessed he came from this kind of wealth.

"Don't get too impressed. Rich people tie their shoes just like everybody else." He squeezed her hand as they pulled up to a free-standing red brick mansion with sash windows and a large fanlight bordering the front door.

"This is beautiful," Ava said in a hushed tone.

"The house was designed by Charles Bulfinch," Tom noted. "A famous architect credited with many historical landmarks in the area."

A man with a bald head and a suit greeted them at the door. "Mr. Tom. Welcome home."

Despite the man's hesitancy, Tom took his hand and gave it a vigorous shake. "It's good to see you, Porges."

After being introduced to Ava, he led them into a large foyer with marble floors. An entry table displayed a massive floral bouquet of yellow rose stems, their fragrance filled the room.

"Your mother is anxiously waiting," Porges told them. He snapped his fingers, and another gentleman appeared. "Take Mr. Tom's and his guest's bags to their rooms, please."

The man nodded and did his bidding.

Ava's insides quivered slightly as she considered this new knowledge. Tom had neglected to reveal this side of his story. She suddenly felt as though she was holding the hand of someone who was suddenly a stranger.

Tom Strobe was a highly skilled golf course architect of the highest reputation. That alone was worth a bit of reverence, but this? This was outside her wildest consideration. The man she'd been falling in love with had a side she'd never considered, never had disclosed to her.

His mother was seated in a room to the right of the foyer. She sat on a period piece ivory sofa holding a single-stick cane in her veined hands.

Tom immediately moved in her direction. "Mother." He bent and drew her into an embrace, one she didn't return.

However, her expression warmed. "Son. Good to see you."

She craned to get a better look at Ava. "You must be Ava Briscoe." She extended her hand. "I'm Frances Strobe."

Ava stepped forward and took the older woman's hand. "It's a pleasure to meet you." She would have liked to have said that she'd heard so much about her. The truth was, she hadn't. This entire chapter of Tom's life was a closed book.

Mrs. Strobe tapped her cane on the velvet-pile carpet. "Come closer. I want to get a good look at you."

Ava held back a frown. She didn't especially like the notion of being inspected. Still, she smiled and moved closer to Tom's mother, well aware her linen slacks had wrinkled during the long flight.

"Tell me—" the old woman said as she gazed up and down. "What is it like to live on an island in the middle of the Pacific Ocean?"

Tom intercepted the question. "We both love it there, Mom. You need to visit. I think you'd enjoy the extraordinary beauty, the fragrant flowers, and the morning showers that leave rainbows painted across the sky."

His mother narrowed her eyes. "Yes, I may have to make a trip."

Tom smiled across at her. "You have a standing invite, Mother."

Ava was taken aback by how the two spoke to one another. Again, this formality was a side of Tom she'd not experienced.

His mother lifted her chin. "I'm sure you are both tired from the trip and would like to freshen up." She looked directly at Ava. "Your room is separate from Tom's, as requested."

Ava cringed. She hadn't considered the implications of her concern, that more than the two of them would know of her decision not to share a bedroom at this juncture of their relationship. It felt...well, a bit exposed.

"Dinner is at seven," his mother announced. "We'll be eating in the dining room overlooking the garden this evening."

Tom and Ava bid her a temporary goodbye. Tom took Ava's hand, and together they made their way back out to the foyer and up a Scarlett O'Hara staircase.

"Why didn't you tell me?" Ava questioned on their way up.

"Tell you?"

Ava's hands made a sweeping motion. "About all this. I didn't know you came from this world." She emphasized the word this to make her point.

Tom let out a little laugh. "If you only knew how little it all means to me. I don't mention all this because Boston is such a small part of my life. It's my past, not my present."

Ava challenged him with a look. "You can say that, Tom. But everyone knows it's impossible to separate ice cream from a milkshake."

24

Ava stood before the floor-length mirror in her ensuite bathroom, worrying that she was underdressed. The mid-length cotton floral dress in shades of teal perfectly matched the thin-strapped sandals on her feet. The drop rattan earrings and bangles complemented the outfit perfectly. Still, a small voice inside told her everyone else, meaning Tom's mother, would be dressed far more elegantly.

She lifted her chin. Where was this self-doubt coming from? She was a confident woman, an accomplished woman. Why was she acting like some school girl on a first date?

Ava sighed. She'd been broadsided and left feeling off-kilter, that's all. After seeing Tom seriously for several months, never once had he revealed that his family dripped cash from their fingertips. She frowned.

What else didn't she know?

Ava was ashamed to admit this, but the minute she entered her room earlier, she'd plopped herself on the bed and grabbed her phone. A quick internet search revealed the extent of his family's prestigious heritage. His family could be traced back to the Boston Tea Party. For generations, his ancestors made large fortunes in the stock market as commodity investors, later rolling over profits by investing in real estate and a wide range of business industries across the United States.

His father had passed away nearly fifteen years prior, leaving his mother at the helm of the family and, more particularly, heading his pet project, the prestigious Exeter Endowment Foundation, one of the largest philanthropic organizations in the nation.

She gulped. Her own father was a doctor and had been considered financially well off by many. His financial statement was dust compared to Tom's family. While money was not everything and certainly was not her guiding light, she was sobered to learn of the influence Tom's family wielded. Quite simply, she was floored by it all.

Why hadn't he told her?

Taking a final glance in the mirror, she took a deep breath and turned to answer the light rap at the door.

"You look amazing," Tom said, placing a kiss against her cheek. "Maybe we can escape after dinner and do some sightseeing. I'm dying to have you alone for more than a few minutes." He grinned suggestively.

"Am I underdressed?" she asked him, seeing that he wore a suit.

"Absolutely not," he firmly told her.

But, of course, she was.

The minute she entered the dining room, she realized they would not be dining with his mother alone. She'd invited guests—guests dressed like they were attending a gala—men in tuxedos and women in knee-length gowns and heels.

She felt like a brown wren in a room of peacocks.

When she'd asked about what clothes to bring on the trip, he'd simply said the celebration would be simple, only a few of their closest friends. Nothing over the top.

If this was a simple dinner, she couldn't imagine the upcoming birthday celebration.

A bald man with a chin-length white mustache greeted them. "Tom," he said, stiffly patting Tom on the shoulder.

"Hello, Myron. It's good to see you."

The two chatted briefly before more guests crossed the room to greet them. Tom made introductions, and Ava shook hands with each person, working on memorizing their names.

Eventually, Tom's mother joined them. Next to her stood a woman with striking features and eyes the color of dark topaz. Her coffee brown hair was swept up in a precise chignon fastened by clips that looked like real diamonds.

Tom shifted uncomfortably.

"Ava, this is Erica."

"Erica Strobe," the woman said, cutting him off.

"His wife," Tom's mother added, the corners of her lips pulling into a shrewd smile.

"Ex-wife," Tom quickly clarified.

Ava blinked several times, trying to absorb the barrage of information and digest what she'd just encountered. This woman was Tom's former wife? And, she was included as a guest at tonight's social event?

Clearly, this gorgeous creature wasn't as former as Ava would have liked. Especially when it came to Tom's mother.

Good sense took over, and Ava recovered from the surprise. She extended her hand. "It's nice to meet you."

"You are the woman who grows the little pineapples on Maui." Tom's ex-wife said this more as a statement than a question.

"Yes," Ava confirmed. "I own Pali Maui." She lifted her chin, refusing to let this situation rattle her nerves. She had nothing to apologize for. Nothing to feel small about. If this were Christel or Katie, she'd take their chins and look them in the eyes. She'd tell them to remember who they were and not compare themselves to anyone, or anything, else. They were more than enough.

Myron cleared his throat. "I believe a shipping company we've invested in distributes for you."

Tom slipped his arm around her waist. "Pali Maui is an immensely successful operation."

Before Ava could add anything, Tom's mother picked up a tiny metal bell from a nearby table and shook it, signaling she wanted everyone's attention.

"Thank you all for joining us this evening. As you know, I'm nearing eighty and who knows how many more opportunities will present to gather with friends? Good parties are not only for the young." She paused and let everyone chuckle. "And it's a rare occasion when my son comes home, so let's all take advantage and enjoy this evening."

They were all seated. To Ava's dismay, she and Tom were directed to chairs next to Erica. In particular, Ava was seated beside her.

In any other setting, she would have found a clever way to protest and amend the situation. This time, she suspected the seating arrangements had been made on purpose, especially when she took her seat and looked directly across the table to find Tom's mother smiling like a Cheshire cat. At that moment, she realized Frances Strobe might be more foe than friend.

"So," Erica said lifting a silver canape fork. "I love your dress."

Ava groaned inside. "Thank you." Under the table, Tom reached for her hand as he engaged in a conversation with the fellow on his other side.

Erica daintily picked at the shrimp cocktail before her. "You must enjoy living on Maui. Tom and I honeymooned there. He loved it. I thought the island was far too crowded with tourists."

Another news bullet that pierced her heart…they'd honeymooned on Maui? Her Maui?

Tom was too busy talking with the guy to notice her drop her own fork. The impact as it hit the dainty fluted plate made a loud clatter that drew everyone's attention. To Ava's horror, there was a tiny crack in the plate.

"Oh, I'm so sorry," She laid her linen napkin on the table hoping to hide the damage. Unfortunately, she couldn't hide her humiliation.

A member of the wait staff was by her side immediately and swept away the evidence. Another staff person set a fresh cocktail plate before her with a canape fork.

Erica smiled, seeming to enjoy Ava's predicament.

The woman dabbed her linen napkin at the corners of her lips. "Tom took me on a day excursion where we shuttled over to an island on a boat. We rented an open-air jeep and we explored the trails. I didn't enjoy being jostled like that, but the views were breathtaking."

Ava stiffened in her chair. "Lana'i," she said.

"What?"

"The island. It's called Lana'i." Memories of the day Tom took her on a similar trip flashed in Ava's mind. While neither had acknowledged the fact at the time, it had been their first real date.

Thankfully, the wait staff appeared and removed the dishes and the main course was served. In order to avoid further interaction with Tom's ex-wife, Ava turned her attention to a man and woman sitting across the table and struck up a conversation.

She learned their names were Ralph and Margaret Emery, good friends of Tom's mother and deceased father. They lived on Nantucket and had flown into Boston for Frances' birthday celebration. "We used to go on day treks in the bay with the Strobe family," Margaret told her. "Ralph taught Tom to sail. Even as a boy, he was a natural and took to tacking almost instantly. We weren't surprised to learn he bought his own sailboat as soon as he grew old enough." Margaret shook her white-haired head. "We hear he hasn't used his yawl in years."

Erica chuckled. "Tom used it plenty when he was here in Boston. We used to go out every weekend. He insisted on teaching me how to raise the sails." She laughed again. "Unfortunately, no matter how patient he was, I couldn't tell the difference between the mainsail and the jib."

Ava closed her eyes. This dinner was fast becoming as entertaining as a dentist appointment. Every time Tom's ex-wife opened her mouth, Ava felt like she was getting a tooth pulled.

Worse, at every opportunity, Tom's mother brought up more inappropriate subjects—even talking ad nauseum about Erica's wedding dress and how the designer was from France. Apparently, the gown was so remarkable that Erica ended up modeling it for a local magazine article featuring brides.

At the long-awaited end of a conversation about a five-week tour she'd taken to Europe with Tom and Erica, Ava realized the ill-suited, and hurtful, topics might be chosen on purpose —that Frances Strobe was not exactly Ava's ally.

It wasn't until much later that evening, after everyone had said their goodbyes, leaving Tom and Ava alone with his mother, that the notion was cemented.

Frances had barely poured herself a brandy when she turned. "Ava, dear. I hope you don't think me rude, but I'd like some time alone with Tom. Would you excuse us?"

The comment hit Ava like a wave, the kind you don't see coming and knocking you off your feet.

She swallowed and looked her nemesis right in the eye. "Absolutely."

Tom protested. "Mother, we can talk in the morning."

Frances was not moved. "Goodnight, Ava. I hope you sleep well."

With that, Ava was dismissed.

She knew better, but something made her hold back just

outside the door. She mentally argued that she wasn't being nosy. The buckle on her sandal simply needed adjusting.

Ava leaned down, knowing her curiosity was overpowering and getting the better of her, but she couldn't seem to stop listening—especially when she heard his ex-wife's name.

If Alani were standing next to her, she knew her best friend would urge her on with this advice. "The destination signs aren't matching the on-ramp here, Ava. I think you'd best drive down this freeway with your eyes and ears wide open and watch for the quickest exit."

"Excuse me, Ms. Briscoe."

The voice made her jump. She turned to find Porges standing beside her with a grim expression. "May I show you to your room?"

"Oh, yes. Thank you." She tried to hide her embarrassment, straightened, and followed him dutifully up the stairs.

25

The following morning Ava asked Tom to take her shopping. "I'd like to go to Viola Lovely," she told him as she handed over the handwritten directions she'd scribbled out the night before. "I read the trendy boutique offers tailored clothing fashioned after shops in Paris."

He looked at her as though she'd grown two heads. "Shopping?"

"Yes," she said firmly. "I want something new to wear tonight." Ava was not about to have a repeat of last night and feel understated at Tom's mother's birthday celebration.

"Sure, we can do that," he responded, pulling her into an embrace. His mouth found its way to hers. She closed her eyes and let herself get lost in the feel of his lips against her own, relishing the intimate moment."

"There you are, Tom."

Startled, Ava pulled back.

His mother stood several feet from them, leaning on her cane. "Tom, I'd like to spend some time with you this morning going over a few things regarding the foundation. We've had some critical developments you need to be aware of."

"I'm sorry, Mother. I just promised to take Ava shopping this morning." He smiled over at her. "Afterward, I'd hoped to take her sightseeing."

"I'm afraid all that must wait," his mother said firmly. "As I said, these are matters of great import." She looked over at Ava. "I'll have the town car brought around. My driver will take you anywhere you'd like."

"Mother, no..." Tom argued.

She stamped her cane. "I won't take no for an answer."

The exchange robbed Ava of breath. She'd never heard anyone talk to Tom in such a manner, nor would she ever have imagined Tom allowing such disrespect.

"That's all right, Tom. You stay and I'll be fine shopping solo. Really."

She waited for his response, mentally relishing him turning down her offer and putting his mother in her place.

To her dismay, her desired retort did not come.

Instead, Tom squeezed her hand. "I'm sorry, Ava. Let me attend to all this and then I'll meet you for lunch. We'll go touring after?"

She sniffed. "Sure. That would be fine." She avoided looking at his mother, afraid of the victory she'd see there. Few people climbed up Ava's wrong side. Despite dependency on a cane, Frances Strobe seemed to scale boundaries just fine.

For good measure, Ava pasted a smile and directed her gaze across at her nemesis. "I'm grateful, actually. Shopping with men can be painful." She widened her smile to cement her declaration and hide how miffed she'd become at this woman.

"Good. It's settled then." Frances looped her arms through Tom's and led him away, chattering about an upcoming board meeting.

Ava stood there, speechless.

What had just happened?

She wasn't used to succumbing to a strong and often rude

female who thrust her way in every situation. Life was far too short to put up with awful people.

Ava shook her head. The Tom she'd met and grown fond of was nothing like his mother. He was kind, thoughtful, and generous to a fault. She could never have imagined him being related to someone so pushy and self-important. No amount of money excused ill manners.

Despite the disappointing turn of events, Ava determined not to let Frances Strobe ruin her morning. She ignored the offer of the car and stubbornly called an Uber.

Viola Lovely was everything it was described to be. The store was located in what was known as the South End of Boston and featured trendy yet sophisticated clothing. Ava easily found a perfect garment for the evening celebration, a sleeveless blush-colored floor-length dress with simple flowing lines featuring a sheer fabric overlaying the skirt. The dress reminded her of a Carolina Herrera design Christel had shown her on the internet.

Ava chose shoes that were sling pumps with kitten heels, then she picked out a drop chain necklace with a pendant made of mother of pearl and matching earrings. The outfit was elegant yet understated.

Despite the earlier tension, Ava smiled to herself as the lady behind the counter took the address and promised to have the purchases delivered in plenty of time for the party. The time spent shopping had been very enjoyable. She didn't miss Tom, really. It had been a long while since she'd spent time alone, and rarely had she traveled solo. She actually liked being by herself.

Ava had endured a lonely marriage, and in the months following Lincoln's death, she'd found her way as a widow who lived alone. She appreciated that her family all lived near her and relished every moment with them and dear friends. Yet, it was an easy jump to evenings spent curled up with a good book and a glass of wine. Ava liked her own company and had no problem entertaining herself.

So much so that she failed to notice the time or the fact Tom had neglected to reach out so they could meet up and see some sights, as he'd promised. When he did call, he sounded frantic.

"I am so sorry, Ava. Please forgive me. I never meant to skip our afternoon together. I'm afraid Mother's agenda was lengthy. One thing led to another, and well..."

"Please, don't worry," she assured him. "I had a lovely afternoon."

"Where are you now?" he asked.

"I've just called an Uber, and I'll be heading back your way."

That seemed to please him. "Excellent. Let's plan on having a glass of wine together before heading to the restaurant for the party."

"That sounds lovely," she told him. reminding herself that the key to being happy was knowing she had the power to choose what to accept and what to let go.

This trip to Boston had been filled with disappointment. She didn't have to allow that to ruin her attitude.

The sage words of her brother's advice in the aftermath of Lincoln's betrayal reminded her that her attitude was in her hands alone. No one else could dictate her happiness unless she chose to abdicate her joy.

Frances held her birthday party at a rooftop venue overlooking the John F. Kennedy Presidential Library and the harbor. Linen-draped tables were perched among pots overflowing with grace roses and ranunculus with stringed lights draped overhead. A string quartet played while white-gloved servers passed trays of champagne and caviar crème fraîche tartlets.

The guest list of hundreds left Ava hopeful she might not run into Erica again this evening.

She was wrong.

"Well, hello." Erica looped her arm with Tom's. "Your mother tells me you got all the details worked out this afternoon."

The comment wedged itself between Ava's shoulder blades. Never one to be possessive or jealous, she still found the exchange bothersome. She did not particularly like that Tom had a continuing relationship with his ex-wife, or that his former mate was privy to and lauded around information like she was still married to him. There may be a divorce decree in place but Ava was learning Erica Strobe was still considered part of this family.

Worse? Tom had glossed entirely over the fact by providing only the barest of information when the subject of his divorce had come up.

Unbidden memories of Lincoln's secrets and illicit connection to another woman barged into her sensibility. Her thoughts were rash, she knew. Still, she couldn't help feeling a parallel to the current situation.

Tom turned uneasy, and his voice strained. "We're at a party, Erica. Let's not discuss business."

Erica's eyes flashed with anger. Just as quickly, her face morphed into capitulation. "Of course, you're entirely right, Tom." She turned to face Ava. "Please accept my apologies. It's never acceptable to discuss family business in mixed company."

Erica reached out a perfectly manicured hand and patted Ava on the arm. "I hope you two have a lovely evening." Her words dripped with insincerity.

Ava could no longer stay quiet. The minute she and Tom were out of hearing range, she brought the subject up. "What was all that about?" she whispered, a bit more tersely than intended.

Tom pulled two champagne flutes from a tray held by a server. "It's nothing, really."

Just like that, Tom Strobe crossed over. Like Lincoln, he evaded her questions and tried to make light of her concerns.

And, just like that, Ava's wall went up. She had a closet of Scrabble and Connect Four at home, if Tom wanted to play games. Ava had made her mind up long ago that she would never be played again.

Never.

26

Christel closed down the internet and shut her laptop, then leaned back into the pillows on her bed, fighting mental exhaustion.

She'd spent days researching all the possibilities, the likely journey ahead. With Evan's password, she had access to even more portals than would be available to the general public. After days of rifling through articles, blogs, and scientific studies, all she could see ahead was a sea of tests and procedures that might not even be effective... surgeries, IVFs, FETs, experimental treatments, second opinions, third opinions...more cycles, more debt.

If the decision were solely up to her, she might choose to pass on all of it. Did she really need to be a mother to feel complete? She had a good life filled with people she cared deeply about, a career that she found more than satisfying. She lived on Maui, for goodness sake, where the rolling ocean and swaying palms were an everyday occurrence.

Sure, she hoped to have children someday, but this striving was exhausting. All this stress of trying to get pregnant.

Something deep inside told her nature would take its

course and it would happen, given time. While she knew it was not his intention, Evan's announcement made her feel rushed and pressured.

He wanted to start a family and didn't want to wait. His expectations weighed heavy on her soul and robbed her of the carefree joy she'd known in the days following their surprise wedding.

Christel simply wanted to return to how it was before when she woke each morning and her lack of pregnancy was not the first thing to hit her mind.

As if on cue, her phone rang. It was Evan.

"Honey, good news! I pulled some professional strings, and we have an appointment to have you seen on Friday. Dr. Varghese is the best fertility specialist around, and she made room in her schedule. In fact, she reminded me this delay is often seen in couples of our age." He let out a chuckle. "I guess my being over forty means we're officially middle-aged and no longer spring chickens. Remember when we were teens, had sex, and tried everything we knew to avoid getting pregnant? Now, we're willing to pay the price of a month-long trip to Europe to spot a tiny fetus in an ultrasound." He grinned widely. "I'm so glad Dr. Varghese could see us so quickly."

Her husband was rambling gleefully. Trying to match his enthusiasm, Christel swallowed her angst and simply replied, "I agree. That's wonderful, honey."

As promised, Dr. Varghese saw them in her office a few days later. The fertility center where she practiced was in Honolulu. They boarded an island jumper, one of the small planes that transported people between islands, and found themselves sitting in her waiting room well before the appointed time.

"I feel really good about this, Christel. I've talked to a lot of colleagues and..."

"You discussed my inability to get pregnant with co-workers?"

He brushed off her concerns with a look. "That's not uncommon in my field. No physician practices in a bubble. We are constantly seeking out the counsel of doctors who specialize outside our own fields." He said it as if that put the matter to rest.

"That may be, but this is my personal issue. I don't relish having my non-performing ovaries and lack of fertile eggs bantered around as lunchtime fodder."

"You're being silly." He reached for a magazine from the table next to where he sat. Evan scanned the cover and tossed the issue aside, then grabbed another. After a quick glance, he cast the magazine on top of the discarded pile. "Remind me when we get home to talk with Evelyn and see that she has current magazine issues in my waiting room."

"Are you nervous?" Christel asked.

"Nervous? No, why?" He rubbed at the side of his tanned face. "Well, maybe a little," he admitted. "I just want this so badly, you know?"

Yes, she did know.

A rotund woman with red hair appeared holding a clipboard. "Mr. and Mrs. Matisse?"

Evan jumped up. "Yes, that's us."

Christel sighed. Who else would it be? They were the only couple in the waiting room.

They both stood and followed the woman back to an examination room. Christel was told to strip down and don a gown tied in the back.

The door opened and a woman who looked a lot like Kate Middleton, the Duchess of Cambridge, entered wearing a white coat and a warm smile. She extended a hand to Evan. "You must be Dr. Matisse."

"Yes. Thank you for making time to see us."

"It's my pleasure. Now, let's see what we've got here."

Over the next hours, Christel was placed on a hard table

with her feet in metal stirrups. She suffered the indignity of an examination. Blood was drawn. Urine samples were provided. She answered dozens and dozens of questions. Many Evan answered before she could provide the information.

When they'd finally finished, Dr. Varghese told Christel she could get dressed, and they were instructed to meet her in her office.

Unlike Evan's office, Dr. Varghese had chosen a chrome and glass desk. The chairs were made of white leather, and animal skins covered the floor. "I am an avid hunter," she explained when she noticed Christel looking. "I go on annual safari to the Serengeti."

She slipped into the chair behind her desk. "We've assumed Evan's sperm count is sufficient, given the history of a prior pregnancy. At this juncture, we are focusing on you, Christel. Of course, that could change, and we'll pivot on our approach if I find it necessary."

The doctor went through all the potential blocks to their getting pregnant. "We don't find evidence of endometriosis, your ovaries do not appear to be polycystic, and there seems to be adequate function in your fallopian tubes. From what I see, there are no glaring reasons you are having difficulty. Given that, the diagnosis is as I suggested to you earlier."

Evan frowned. "Meaning?"

"My best professional assessment is that age may be a factor. For women over thirty-five, it can take longer to get pregnant."

"My wife is only thirty-four." He turned to Christel. "Isn't that right, honey?"

She nodded.

"Many women assume if they still get regular periods, their fertility is fine, but that isn't necessarily true," Dr. Varghese explained. "Age impacts egg quality as well as quantity."

Christel felt her hands grow sweaty. "So, what do we do?"

Dr. Varghese glanced between them. "You keep trying. Given these initial findings, it is my professional opinion that you will get pregnant...in time." She smiled. "In the meantime, enjoy trying."

Evan rubbed the back of his neck. "Well, my wife has been wigged out about all this. I suppose stress can hinder the process as well."

Christel scowled. "I'm not stressed," she argued.

He shrugged. "Well, regardless. These results couldn't have turned out any better." He stood and shook hands with Dr. Varghese. "Thank you so much. And if there is ever anything I can do for you, please don't hesitate to reach out. I'm good at fixing broken bones," he reminded with a laugh.

Christel's mood turned unusually surly as they gathered their things and headed for the lobby. She had been on this precipice for days, teetering on the fine edge of losing it.

Evan had better tread lightly. She was not old, and she was not stressed.

If her husband pushed any farther and continued to lay blame at her feet, he'd be the one needing an orthopedic surgeon to fix his broken legs.

At the very least, he'd be making their baby alone.

While she didn't use those exact sentiments, she conveyed that message to Evan the minute they were home.

"Evan, you need to know I'm done."

His eyebrows shot up. "Done? I'm not following."

She reached for his hand to soften the blow. "No more tests. No more little wands painted with disappointment. No more obsessing and stressing. All of that is over."

"You...you don't want to get pregnant?"

"I didn't say that. I'm saying I'm no longer hanging a lantern on my shame. Every month I face the prospect of letting you down. Every thirty days or so, I'm crushed with the knowledge that you will wear that look of disappointment. It's too much."

She squeezed his hand. "I do still want to get pregnant. But no more striving, or obsessing. If it happens naturally, we'll rejoice. But no more tears and anxiety. God will create a baby in my womb if it's meant to be." She looked at him, hoping he realized she was only trying to point out the situation as it was.

As the words left her mouth, she felt something rise in her, making her strong. "I love you, Evan. I hope that is enough."

Evan closed the space between them, his chest brushing hers as he looked down and took her chin in his hand. He kissed her once, gently, his lips so full and soft she felt herself leaning into him. Then he backed away and held her gaze long enough to say, "You are always enough, Christel. I'm so sorry if I put added pressure on you. That was never my intent." He tucked a curl behind her ear with a determined look. "Even if God never gives us a baby, he has already given me far more than I deserve."

Evan turned and took her in his arms. He folded her close and laid a kiss on the crown of her head, the place where her hair curved along the line of her high forehead.

His grin came back. "I have an idea. Let's go have some "no-baby-making sex." He scooped her up in his arms and headed for the bedroom.

Laughter rose through her and spilled out in a light, airy sound of pure joy. "Why, Dr. Matisse, I thought you'd never ask."

27

Ava folded her blouse and placed it into the suitcase. She glanced around the room to ensure she hadn't forgotten anything, then snapped the suitcase shut, glad this little excursion to see Tom's mother was nearing an end.

A rap at the door caught her attention. "I'll be right there, Tom." She grabbed her bag and headed for the door. To her surprise, the person on the other side was not Tom. It was his mother.

"Good morning, Ava," Frances said, leaning over her cane. Even at this time of the morning, the woman looked elegant. Her silver hair was swept up into curls stylishly clipped behind one ear. She wore a two-piece pantsuit in a pretty violet shade. The color matched her eyes. "I'd like a moment before you leave."

Ava took a deep breath and stepped back, bracing herself. "Come in."

"Thank you," Frances said. She moved into the room and stood by a large paned window overlooking her garden. "I love

Shasta daisies. They are such happy flowers. I don't suppose you have daisies in Maui, do you?"

"I believe they grow wild on the drier side of the island, near the volcanic landscapes."

Frances turned and looked Ava directly in the eyes. "I'm sure you are on a tight schedule and I know you and my son have a plane to catch soon, so let me cut to the chase." She lifted her chin slightly. "Few people know I was not my husband's first choice as a wife."

Ava frowned, puzzled by the direction of this conversation.

"He was in love with a girl from Texas. He met her during a debate at the University of Texas at Austin. She was smart as a whip and was studying international law. And the girl was pretty... blonde with slim long, tan legs. Bruno was completely smitten."

Frances tipped her head slightly. "Unfortunately, she was not his kind."

"Not his kind?"

"Her father was a pastor of a small church in a dusty east Texas town. Her mother waitressed at a tiny café, the sort with red vinyl banquettes and sticky breakfast menus."

"I'm sorry, what does this have to do with—"

Frances held up an open palm. "The Strobe family is an American institution. Historically, their prominence was felt in politics on both sides of the aisle. They served on the boards of universities and businesses across the country. Tom's ancestral grandfather helped form the Securities and Exchange Commission and directed many of the economic policies this nation has now come to rely on. With that kind of influence comes immense responsibility. And sacrifice."

Tom's mother paused, letting the information sink in. "Tom has responsibilities."

Ava simply looked at her and remained silent. While there were subtleties in her diatribe, Ava listened carefully and did not want to miss the point of the conversation. If lucky, she'd catch a clue as to why she'd received such a chilly reception.

A hint of dismay crossed the woman's face. "You may be lovely, but you are not what Tom needs."

The statement startled Ava. "I—I'm sorry. I'm not sure I understand."

"As I said, my son has responsibilities. As an only child, Tom is in succession to carry on the family legacy. In particular, he is a benefactor of our beloved Exeter Endowment Foundation and is charged with carrying on our very important work. Organizations slowly die without someone at the helm, a figurehead, and a strong leader. I'm eighty years old. It's time Tom moved into his place, his familial destiny."

"I'm not sure what all this has to do with me," Ava remarked, having difficulty hiding her annoyance.

"My son is fond of you. Very fond. A mother can tell. Yet like my Bruno, romantic happiness is an illusion. Tying one's heart to a bad situation is…well, not wise."

"Are you implying I am a bad situation?" Ava could barely believe what she was hearing.

"I'm sure you are a lovely woman, Ava. Obviously, you are hard-working and accomplished. To clarify, your connection to my son is not optimum. To be even more direct, I want you to break off your relationship."

Ava's hands drew into tight fists at her side. "But, why? What threat do I pose?"

"My son is not enamored with Boston and everything it holds. Long ago, he escaped following his passion for golf. I allowed his temporary ventures, feeling my son needed to sow his oats. I watched with mild interest as his career flourished and he traversed the country building gold courses, ultimately ending up in Maui. A lovely island, to be sure. A romantic place filled with notions of sunsets and lore."

Frances' eyes turned to steel. "However, the time has come

for Tom to wake from his dream. He must return to Boston and his responsibilities. You are a hindrance, a distraction, to that end."

Ava's hand flew to her chest. "You think I have that kind of power over Tom? You are wrong about that. First, your son and I are friends. Dear friends. Romantically involved, yes. But you overestimate our involvement." Ava gathered more air into her lungs. "Further, Tom is a grown man—a man I've come to know fairly well. I highly suspect you have also overestimated any woman's influence over him. That includes me, and more so, you."

Ava jabbed her finger toward the nasty woman with her perfectly coifed hair. "Finally, you highly overestimate my tolerance for your rudeness."

Frances slowly and silently moved forward. "If I have failed to communicate the entirety and extent of my concerns, let me now clarify and leave no question remaining. It has also come to my attention that you are having financial difficulties...a mother must look out for her son's interests, even when he seems unable to see what is before his eyes."

The comment stabbed.

"If you mean to imply that I am after your son's financial resources, you are sorely mistaken. Until this weekend, I was totally unaware..."

Tom suddenly appeared in the open doorway. "There's my girls." He looked at Ava. "Are you ready, sweetheart?"

Ava's eyes burned with unshed tears. She had never been so insulted in all her life. She turned to Tom. "Yes. Let's go, please."

He looked between Ava and his mother. He would have to be dead not to sense the thick tension that now blanketed the room.

He opened his mouth to say something, then must have thought better of the idea. Instead, he reached for Ava's hand.

"The car is waiting. We'll grab breakfast at the airport." He cautiously proceeded to his mother's side and brushed a light kiss against her cheek.

"Think about everything I said," she told him. "I'll call you at the end of the week."

Tom drew a deep breath and exhaled with a heavy sigh. "I will."

"It was good to meet you, Ava," Frances said, leaning over her cane as they gathered her things and moved for the door. "I hope you have a good return trip back to Maui."

28

Ava and Tom were in the town car only moments before she blew up, not caring that the driver would overhear. "I have a few questions," she said with a raised voice, barely able to hold back the entirety of her anger.

Tom quickly grabbed her hand. "Ava, what's the matter?" He appeared truly confused. "Are you talking about that little exchange I just had with my mother? It's not entirely what it seems, sweetheart. I know how to handle my mother—going toe-to-toe with her only fuels the fire. I've learned over time that the best way to douse her intentions is to let her think she's won...walk away, and allow her to believe her demands will be met. She'll learn soon enough that nothing she had to say swayed my thinking or any decisions I make."

"Why didn't you tell me about your family and wealth? Or that you were still connected with your ex-wife—that she would be a guest for dinner and the birthday celebration? You could have at least warned me that I would be face-to-face with your former wife."

He squeezed her hand as they pulled away from his mother's home. "I deeply apologize for that. Frankly, I didn't know

Erica would be there," he confessed. "It wasn't until Mother outlined her plans that her surprise appearance made sense."

"Which are?" Ava demanded.

"What?"

"What plans include your ex-wife?" Her words dripped with irritation. She was not happy about the idea of sharing Tom with 'the other woman.' Not even when a divorce decree existed.

Tom drew a deep breath and held it for several seconds before responding. "I am not at liberty to say. However, I can tell you this—Erica will hold a position at the foundation. My late father's trust dictates that situation, not me and not my mother. Hopefully, that makes the undesirable scenario a bit more palatable." He focused his gaze, looking extremely uncomfortable. "You're important to me, Ava. I hope that eases your mind."

Ava crossed her arms tightly across her chest. "I don't know, Tom. Should I find it palatable that you honeymooned on Maui with your ex-wife and never mentioned the fact, or that you took her to Lana'i and jeeped around the island, just like our first date? Oh, and I found it fascinating that her wedding dress was sewn with over seven-thousand seed pearls, and the satin for the sleeves was flown in directly from Italy." Ava couldn't help it. She punched his arm in earnest. "Really, Tom?"

Instinctively, he reached for her, but she pulled away. "Ava, you have to believe how sorry I am. Truly."

"Sorry doesn't always fix things, Tom."

Tears burned at her eyes. "You hid things from me, Tom. Important things. Sure, I needn't be privy to your family's personal business. But I should not feel blindsided by a whole side of you I never knew existed. And I should be made aware of situations that are sure to make me uncomfortable. How do you think it made me feel when your mother cornered me and told me I was not only a threat, a distraction—but she feared I was after your money?"

Tom's eyes darkened. "She said that?"

"And more." Ava angrily wiped at her eyes. "Your ex-wife is another gem. Bet we're going to be best friends, Erica and me." Sarcasm wasn't usually a tool she wielded, but today, all bets were off.

"I'm a grown woman, Tom. I like my life. I don't need these complications."

His expression filled with worry. "Please, I had no idea the extent to which my mother and Erica crossed the line. They had no right to behave in that manner towards you. Believe me, both of them will hear from me. And soon."

Outside the car window, tree-lined streets turned to billboards as they neared the freeway.

He reached and brushed her hair back from her cheek. "I will make this right. I assure you those two have little—no, they have nothing to do with you and me. Nothing."

"Your mother expects you to return to Boston."

"My mother's list of expectations is long. I've become very practiced at maneuvering her supposition that my life is hers to mold and direct." He looked at her then, with a reassurance she needed to see. "Nothing is going to change, Ava. I am not returning to Boston. That said, I will fulfill the duties my father dictated in his trust. I can do all that is required from Maui, or not at all. Except for the public annual charity event, I can do everything that needs to be done online."

Tom's voice tightened with emotion. "Ava, I assure you, my increased involvement in the Exeter Foundation will have no impact on our relationship whatsoever." He paused meaningfully. "Don't misunderstand. I loved my father and want nothing more than to carry out his wishes. Despite that, I will not up-end my life and grow miserable trying to comply with what my mother so fondly refers to as "family obligations."

Ava appreciated what Tom had to say, yet nothing could erase the unease she now felt. She'd been a fool to rush into another relationship. She needed time...time to secure her life and heal. Clearly, she still carried the trauma of Lincoln and Mia's betrayal and had no reserve left to deal with what was before her now.

She gave Tom a weak smile.

Yes, she needed time and some space. She needed to think all this through.

Ava had a hard time visualizing moving forward with Tom under these circumstances. No matter his excuses, or assurances, he'd reserved telling her the entire story until the situation had forced him to open up and reveal his other side.

Even if not by his hand, she'd been left her dangling above the sharks. His mother and ex-wife still had influence, and she didn't want to live vying for first place in his life.

Yes, he guaranteed nothing they said or did mattered to him. But did she want to be the wedge that came between Tom and his mother?

He promised he had everything handled, that nothing had changed. Ava was sure he wanted to believe every word from his mouth.

Only time would prove if that were true.

29

Tom and Ava rode in silence for over a mile before Tom suddenly leaned forward and tapped the driver on the shoulder. "Turn around, please. We wish to return to my mother's."

Ava's eyes flew open. "What are you doing?"

"We going back. I'm going to settle this with my mother."

"Now? But we'll miss out flight."

"We'll book another," he told her. "Or I'll arrange for a private jet and charter a trip back to Maui."

"Tom, get serious. That would be cost-prohibitive."

Tom's face broke into the tiniest of smiles. "I can afford it."

After a few minutes of mindless argument, Ava gave in. Tom meant business, and nothing she could say would sway his decision.

"I hope you don't mind if I remain in the car," she said as their driver took an off-ramp. "I want no part of this."

"Oh, no." Tom shook his head firmly. "You are the biggest part of this."

The return trip seemed to take no time, and they were again

heading down tree-lined streets. The car came to a stop in front of Frances' elegant home.

"Wait here," Tom told the driver as he helped Ava from the back seat.

They made their way up the cobblestone walkway to the front entrance. Before Tom could ring the bell, the door opened. Porges lifted his bushy eyebrows in surprise. "Mr. Tom?"

Tom pulled Ava into the front foyer, where several uniformed women were changing the bouquet on the table. "Could you please summon my mother?"

A few moments later, Frances appeared. "Tom?"

Tom pointed to the adjoining room. "We need to speak. Privately."

After entering the room, Tom closed the door. "I've been made aware of a situation that highly angers me, Mother."

Frances' expression turned to stone. Ava noticed her knuckles turn white as her grip on the cane tightened, but she said nothing.

"How dare you accuse Ava of being avaricious. Do you really think she is after my money? The wealth she knew nothing about until we arrived in Boston?" His voice thundered. "You owe my dear friend an apology, and I demand you correct this grave error in judgment...right here, right now."

Ava wanted to shrink into the floor. This angry side of Tom was yet another surprise. She'd never seen him lose his temper.

Frances' posture stiffened. Her lips pinched together briefly before she dipped her head in a slight nod. "Of course." She directed her gaze to Ava. "Perhaps I was hasty in my judgment. As you might understand, I have become very protective of my son over the years. You might not have ill intentions, but plenty of wolves out there would like a bite of the Strobe apple."

"An apology, Mother," Tom reminded, his voice still terse.

A pinched, tension-filled expression immediately crossed

his mother's face. "Ava, may I offer you my sincerest apology? I'm sorry."

Ava held her breath. What was she supposed to say?

She simply nodded and said nothing. Extending a verbal acceptance to a forced apology seemed as disingenuous as the voiced regret.

Tom immediately softened. He went to his mother's side and brushed a kiss against her cheek. "Thank you, Mother." Then, as an additional warning, he added, "We won't need another discussion of this sort, will we?" It was not a question.

They were back in the car and headed back to the airport in no time. Tom used his cellphone and booked another flight, one that was scheduled to depart only an hour later than the original but had a layover in Dallas instead of direct.

It was a small price to pay for the extreme satisfaction that filled her. Tom had capitulated and stood up for her. He had drawn firm boundaries that she doubted his mother would dare cross in the future.

While still bothered by how Tom revealed his family wealth, Ava now felt less reticent to let it go.

This was precisely what she confided to Alani the following week.

"Oh, Ava. I'm sorry to hear you and Tom hit a road bump." Her friend shook her scarf-wrapped head. "Relationships are messy. The closer you become to a man, the greater chance your heart will suffer a nick, now and then. Tom is a good man. He cares for you very much, as evidenced by his quick reaction to his mother's outrageous behavior."

"He did let the old bat have it." She reached for the watering can and let a stream of water shower a potted anthurium.

Alani tossed her head back from where she sat on the patio and laughed. "Yes, it sounds like he did."

Ava picked some dead leaves off another potted plant on the table. "I just wished Tom would have told me earlier that his family had that kind of wealth. It was startling to learn by driving up to a house that rivaled the Kennedy compound."

"But he did tell you. He wasn't hiding anything, Ava. Tom took you to Boston. He wouldn't have if he didn't want you to know. I'm sure you would have preferred to learn of it earlier, but I urge you to let that go."

Ava straightened. "Alani, the Strobe family is so affluent, they have their own charitable foundation. Now, that's uber-rich."

"You know as well as I do, it's not about what you look like, your job, or how wealthy you are." Alani lifted her face to the sun. "It's about having people in your life that you love and who love you...that's all that matters."

Ava nodded. "I won't argue that."

Her friend closed her eyes and grinned. "The bigger revelation is that Tom Strobe appears to be in love with you."

30

The day of the grand re-opening of the Pali Maui golf course dawned sunny and bright, as was typical for this time of year on Maui. Tom was not surprised that travel magazines had voted Maui as the best island in the U.S. for more than twenty years. The year-round warm temperatures, ranging from the low sixties at night to high eighties during the day, offered travelers the perfect weather for any adventure, especially those who golf.

"Where do you want the leaderboards, Tom?"

He patted the guy on the back. "Let's erect one at the ninth hole and one at the finish, where people lunching on the deck at No Ka 'Oi will have a direct view of the scores as the tournament players complete the eighteenth hole."

"You got it, boss."

Tom stood with his hands on his hips, surveying the view with great satisfaction. Despite suffering significant setbacks caused by the storm, the course renovation had turned out even better than he'd hoped.

It would be unimaginable for golf enthusiasts worldwide to come to Maui and miss out on playing here at Pali Maui. The course's eighteen holes were carefully designed with wide fairways and generous greens, dramatic ocean views, and stunning mountain scenery, making it an enjoyable play for the average golfer while remaining a challenge for celebrated professionals. He'd already been contacted by Tiger Wood, Vijay Singh, and Ernie Els, all anxious to book the newest golf adventure on the island.

Today was the debut launch of the Ava Briscoe Annual Golf Tournament. The tournament player line-up filled as soon as the event was formally announced and the venue was buzzing with activity. Tents were being erected, as well as audience stands and last-minute preparations.

Grounds volunteers were putting finishing touches on every hole, even placing planters filled with tropical blooms at each tee box along with coolers filled with ice and complimentary cold beverages.

Of all the projects he'd worked on, this had been Tom's favorite. Not only was the design a challenge given the terrain, but he'd encountered a woman he found fascinating—a woman he could see himself spending the rest of his life with.

Admitting that truth caused tiny tremors to run down his spine. He'd never been good at expressing his feelings but had gotten damn good at feeling them since he'd found Ava.

The very idea of her brought a smile to his face.

Ava Briscoe was unlike any woman he had ever known. Intelligent, funny, wise, and, oh, so beautiful. He couldn't recall ever knowing a woman whose hair he wanted to stroke, to lie in, to bury his face in.

She was his first thought in the morning, the last before he shut his eyes and drifted to sleep...and every thought in between.

No notion was as crushing as the one where he feared losing her—which was why the trip to Boston continued to haunt him.

How could he have been so stupid to not alert her of what was to come, of his family's wealth...and how difficult his mother could be when she was driven by a notion she couldn't let loose of?

He'd meant to protect her, to refrain from overwhelming her with the knowledge that his family was prominent and wealthy beyond imagination...ease her into learning of that side of his life. His plans had backfired, and she'd ended up wounded.

He would never forgive himself for the pain on Ava's face as she told him what she had endured at the hands of his mother and ex-wife. His blood boiled even now, thinking about it. Tom was not surprised to learn that Erica had been catty and mean. His ex-wife had many qualities he detested. Jealousy and arrogance were two at the top of the list.

He also knew his mother could be cunning and ruthless. Typically, she utilized that side of her persona for her business negotiations. He shouldn't be shocked that, according to Frances Strobe, everything was a business deal.

In any event, his mother was smart enough to hear his message and absorb it. He would never tolerate malicious avarice directed towards the woman who had captured his heart. If forced to choose, his mother would not like the outcome.

"Tom!"

He heard his name called and turned around. Ava walked toward him, followed by her family—Christel and Evan, Jon and Katie, their two girls, and Aiden. Shane carried his little son, Carson. Captain Jack sauntered not far behind the group, chewing on a cigar. He pushed Alani in a wheelchair.

Elta gasped. "Hey, be careful," he warned as Jack popped his wife into a wheely and spun her around.

Alani laughed and waved off her husband's caution. "Settle down, my love. He's not going to drop me on the ground."

In the distance, Vanessa climbed from her car. She waved and hurried to join them.

Tom grinned and moved to Ava's side. In a bold move, he took her fragile, beautiful face into his hands and kissed her, slowly and thoroughly—not caring that dozens of eyes watched.

"Whoo-hoo!" Shane shouted while the rest of her family applauded.

"Get a room," Willa added with a big smile.

Flushed, Ava pulled back. She slapped at his chest. "Tom!" she said in protest but smiled. "Not in front of the children."

"What did I miss?" Vanessa asked, breathless, as she reached the group. She glanced around. "I repeat, what did I miss?"

Ava smiled at Tom, then looked over at the others, her heart full and overflowing.

The past few months had been rough, riddled with disappointment, insurmountable obstacles, and, sometimes, crippling doubt and fear. Yet, throughout the ups and downs, the sunny days and the storms—these were the ones who always remained by her side, the ones she loved more than her own life.

She squeezed Tom's hand.

"You are my Ohana," she announced, beaming. "The people who make my life worth living—my family."

She filled her lungs with sweet island air, letting laughter rise through her and spill out in a light, airy sound of pure joy.

"I am a blessed woman, indeed."

EPILOGUE

Aloha! Captain Jack here. As you can see, even a hurricane-force storm can't take down my sister and her family. Together, they worked like mad to keep their beloved pineapple plantation financially afloat, even holding monthly live concerts at Pali Maui to raise much-needed cash.

Speaking of whirlwinds, Mig Nakamoa is sure caught up in a flurry. He's enamored with that new realtor, even watching her favorite soap operas. (Shh..don't tell, but I like to grab a glass of whiskey and catch me an episode of Days of Our Lives every now and again. The women on that show are hot.)

Well, moving on...how heartbreaking to watch our gal, Alani, struggle to fight against that blasted cancer. I have a feeling she's gonna beat it. She's a tough bird who hangs tight to her faith. Have to love a gal who believes.

Me? I've never been one to park my keester on a church pew—only at weddings and funerals. I have been known to tarry on a bar stool now and then. (chuckles)

Ava's love life sure took a hit when she thought her new guy, Tom, wasn't being open. She still carries some baggage over her late husband's secrets, so learning there was a whole other hidden side of this guy sent her spinning. Ha...but my sis sure didn't take any guff off that battle-ax of a mother or from his prissy ex-wife. I was happy to see Tom stand up for her. If he hadn't, I would've had to have a serious chat with my sister about her future with the guy, know what I mean?

Before I go, 'ole Captain Jack wants to thank each and every one of you readers for supporting Kellie and her books. Every review, every email, every social media post applauding her stories...well, it means a lot.

If ever you find yourself in Maui, stop by, and I'll take you on down to the Dirty Monkey and buy you a whiskey as a thank-you.

Anyway, it's time I get back to the Canefire. Tourists who are lining up for a snorkeling trip over to Lanai. Until next time, grab your coconut bra and grass skirt and hula on over and get a copy of the next book in the series—Sweet Plumeria Dawn.

Captain Jack will catch you later. Aloha!

YES, I WANT A COPY OF THE NEXT BOOK!

ACKNOWLEDGMENTS

A special word of thanks to the folks at Maui Pineapple Plantation (waving to Debbie, Lacey, Mary and Ken!) These fine people let me hang with them and see how pineapples are planted, grown and harvested.

Did you know pineapple crowns are planted in the earth by hand? The pineapples take fourteen to fifteen months to grow. Maui is known for wild pigs and if they break through the fencing, they can eat a football field worth of produce in no time.

The Maui Pineapples are picked to order and are the sweetest treat you'll ever pop in your mouth...no, really! I had such a fun time on the tour and learned so much. You guys were so supportive of this series and my heart is filled with gratitude.

Thanks also to Elizabeth Mackay for the fabulous cover designs, to Jones House Creative for my web design, to my editors, proofreaders, and my publishing team, including the fabulous Cindy Jackson. Special thanks to my personal assistant, Danielle Woods. You guys all make this business so much easier, and definitely more fun.

Hugs and gratitude to my best-selling author friend and critique partner, Jodi Vaughn, who made this book so much better.

To all the readers who hang with me at My Book Friends and She's Reading, you are a blast! I can't believe how much fun it is to do those live author chats and introduce you to my author buddies.

Finally, to all my readers. All this is for you!
~ Kellie

A SNEAK PEEK - SWEET PLUMERIA DAWN (MAUI ISLAND SERIES BOOK 6)

Chapter 1

There were few things Ava Briscoe enjoyed more than family gatherings, even those that held a bit of mystery.

Two days ago, her sister showed up at her door with a request. That alone was not unusual. Vanessa typically had a long list of ways others could meet her needs, wishes, and desires. She defined the term globe head—someone who believed the entire world revolved around her.

She tossed her Louis Vuitton on the counter and helped herself to a bottle of sparkling water from Ava's refrigerator. "Okay, here's the deal," she said. "I want the entire family to come over tomorrow night. I have an announcement."

Ava hoped her sister had found a new job. It had been nearly a month since she'd been suddenly terminated from her position as Communications Director and Media Liaison for Jim Kahele's state senator campaign.

Okay, terminated might not be the right word. Actually, Vanessa had quit. Her pride couldn't handle what she considered a demotion when Jim hired a beautiful young woman and made her Campaign Manager. Vanessa claimed she would never report to his girlfriend; never mind that she, too, had dated Jim before going to work for him.

The entire scenario painted a new perspective on the campaign slogan Vanessa had coined—Your Choice for Change.

Truthfully, Ava was saddened to learn Vanessa had lost her dream job. It was not the first time. Her sister had landed in Maui after being asked to vacate her anchor desk at a big news station in Seattle for making a political snafu on air. She loved that job, and she was good at it. Her ability to spin a story and wheedle people into her camp was unsurpassed, which was another reason a political campaign had been right up her alley. Vanessa joked that political campaigning was nothing more than promising to build a bridge, even when there was no river.

Ava leaned against the kitchen counter. "Care to give me a preview of the big announcement?" she asked.

Vanessa vehemently shook her head. "No. It's a surprise. A big one."

Ava folded despite the heavy schedule at Pali Maui and the short notice. "Okay, but I can't promise everyone will be able to make it. You will have to make all the calls because I'm tight on time. We have an important meeting today with an advertising agency. Christel and I decided to explore venturing into a new international social media campaign. The agency promises they can increase our revenues by fifty percent...ambitious in my opinion, but Christel believes we need to hear what they have to say."

"Absolutely," Vanessa agreed. "If you're not willing to plunge forward and embrace new ways of doing things, you will fall victim to lagging behind."

To her surprise, the party came together, and everyone was

in attendance, except Katie's husband, Jon. It was rare that he could leave No Ka 'Oi during the heavy dinner hour. Even on weeknights, his restaurant overlooking the golf course at Pali Maui was booked to capacity. He did promise to have the cooks prepare extra entrées and have Katie deliver them to save Ava needing to prepare food for the get-together. Her son-in-law was thoughtful like that.

Katie was the first to arrive with her teen daughter, Willa, and little Noelle. "So, what is Aunt Vanessa's big news?" she asked while unloading the food.

Ava lifted a box out of Katie's trunk. "I have absolutely no idea." She sniffed the aroma wafting from the closed lid. "Mmm...smells delicious."

"Hamachi tacos. Jon lifted the recipe from Morimoto's menu on their website," she confided. "He duplicated the dish to a tee."

Noelle lifted her chubby little arm in the air. "Me want a taco. Me want a taco."

Katie gave her a patient look. "You have to wait for dinner, sweetheart." She performed a typical mommy maneuver to stave off a meltdown and offered her a substitute. "You can have some pineapple. Maybe Grammy Ava has a little chocolate syrup you can dip the pieces in."

"That sounds healthy," Ava teased.

"Healthy is overrated," Willa chimed in. "Take it from me; you do not want this little girl having a tantrum when she's hungry."

Ava wondered why Katie couldn't simply let her little daughter eat an early dinner, though she didn't say it. She'd learned long ago not to meddle in her adult children's decisions. If she'd done her job and raised them properly, they would make good choices on all the essential things.

Shane was a perfect example. Who would have thought her wild child would embrace the unexpected responsibilities laid at his feet when Aimee showed up at his door with a surprise son? Or, when she flew back to the mainland a short time later, leaving little Carson and a simple note on the counter with little explanation for her sudden departure beyond wanting to make it big in Hollywood?

Her son had stepped up. He'd sold his motorcycle and left his all-nighters behind to be there for his precious little son, proving her adage even more.

All of her kids were proof that good parenting and putting your children first often panned out.

That didn't mean she still didn't have concerns for her children. At times, she worried about Aiden. He was a perfectionist, never allowing himself any latitude to fail. Since his promotion to Chief at the rescue station, those tendencies had magnified. This left little room for a social life. Outside the family and an occasional surfing excursion, her son rarely made time for fun.

Christel confided she and Evan were desperately trying to get pregnant but had put the attempt on hold because of the stress it caused Christel. Her oldest daughter was another one who never allowed herself to fall short on any level. She was prone to being a little high-strung, had made the Dean's List multiple times at Loyola Law School in Chicago, and got her law and CPA licenses, all so she could run the legal and financial aspects of Pali Maui. No slacking with that girl.

Rarely did Christel fail. Ava's heart broke to know her daughter struggled with her inability to become pregnant. Especially since she'd wanted a family when she married Jay. The heartbreak of his addiction and the divorce robbed her of so much, including time. At her current age, things were more difficult in the child-bearing department. Still, as the fertility expert had reported, Christel was not too old and there were no physical findings that would preclude her from pregnancy. It would happen, given time.

They all gathered early in the evening and were seated

around the table, ready to dig into Jon's delicious food when Vanessa could stand it no longer. She stood and clinked a knife against her water goblet.

"Listen up. Big news, everyone."

She paused, waiting for everyone's eyes to be directed her way. She loved to be the center of attraction, and tonight was no exception.

Willa lifted the taco from her plate. "So, what's the big announcement?"

Vanessa paused again to stretch the building of anticipation. Finally, she let her face break into a wide smile. She clasped her hands together, giddy with excitement.

"This morning, I filed my paperwork to run for office, beginning my candidacy. I'm going to run against Jim Kahale and become Hawaii's next state senator!"

YES, I WANT TO ORDER THIS BOOK!

ALSO BY KELLIE COATES GILBERT

THE MAUI ISLAND SERIES
Under The Maui Sky

Silver Island Moon

Tides of Paradise

The Last Aloha

Ohana Sunrise

Sweet Plumeria Dawn

THE PACIFIC BAY SERIES
Chances Are

Remember Us

Chasing Wind

Between Rains

THE SUN VALLEY SERIES
Sisters

Heartbeats

Changes

Promises

LOVE ON VACATION SERIES
Otherwise Engaged

All Fore Love

TEXAS GOLD SERIES

A Woman of Fortune

Where Rivers Part

A Reason to Stay

What Matters Most

STAND ALONE NOVELS

Mother of Pearl

* * *

Available at all retailers

www.kelliecoatesgilbert.com

Made in the USA
Middletown, DE
13 February 2024

49695980R00111